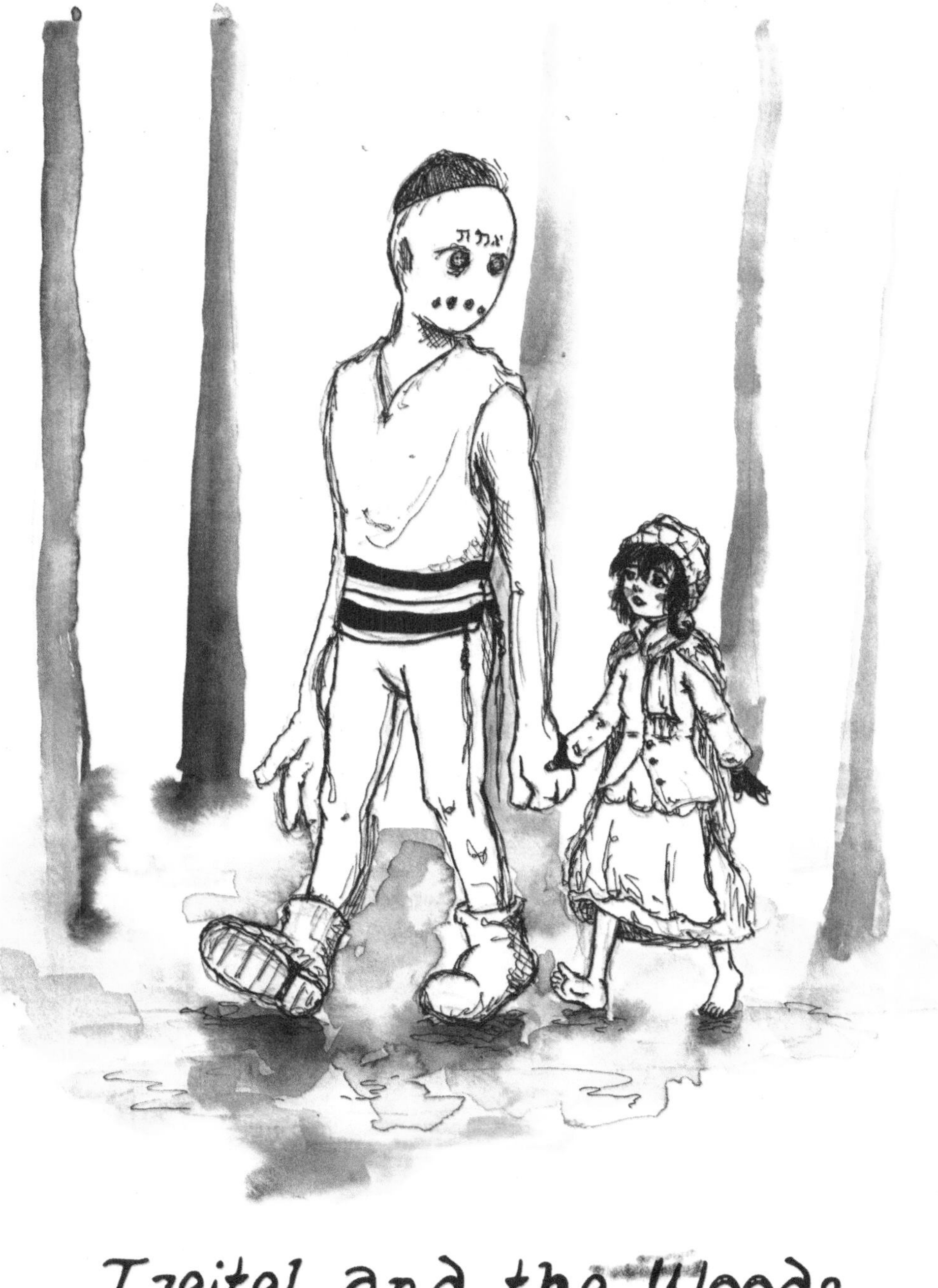

Tzeitel and the Woods

Written and Illustrated by

[redacted]

Ashley Finch

Ashley Finch

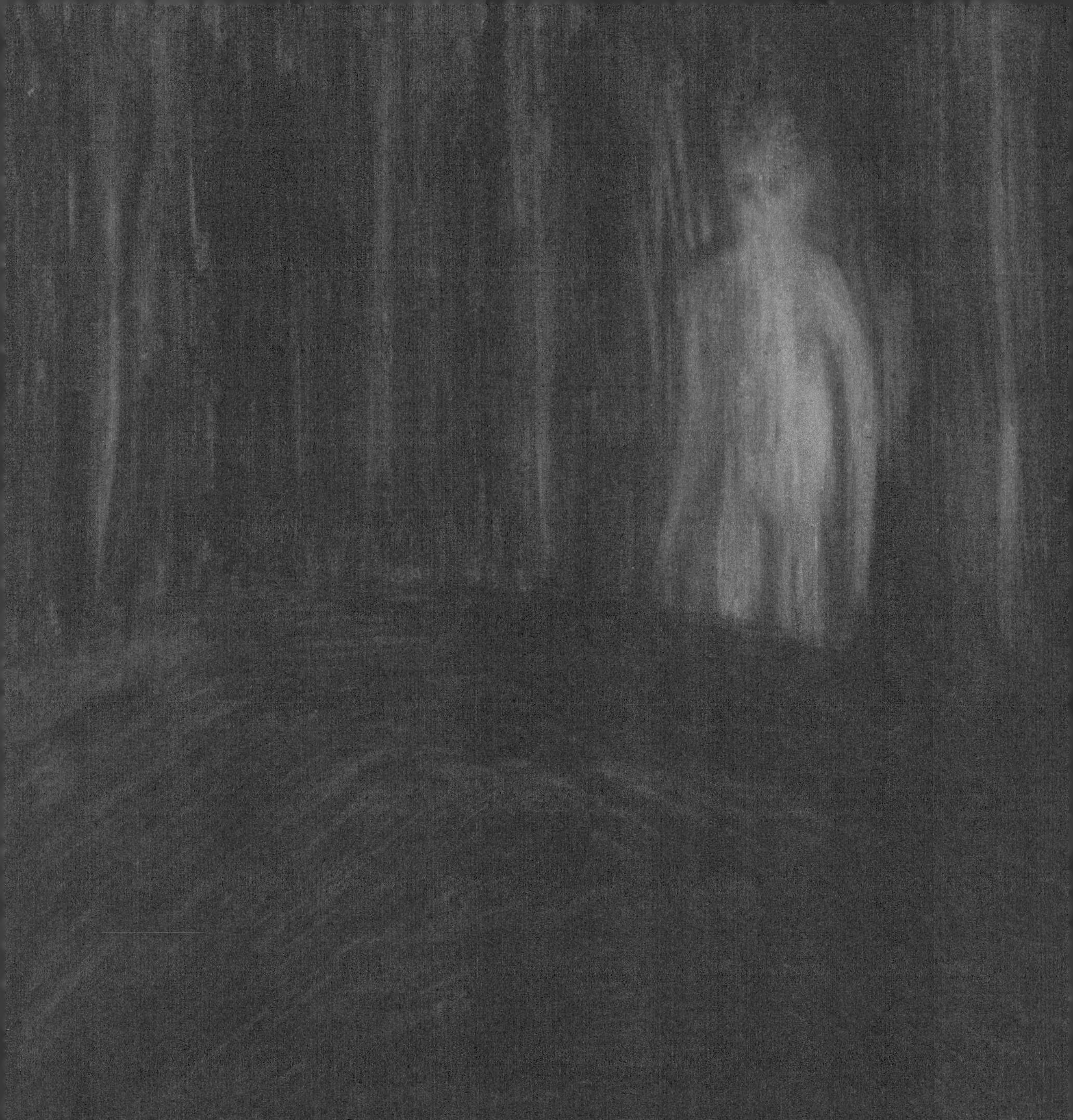

Edited by Louise Pardee

A special thanks to my wife, Cassie. None of this would have been possible without her love, support, and infinite patience.

ISBN-10: 0692239421
ISBN-13: 978-0-692-23942-1

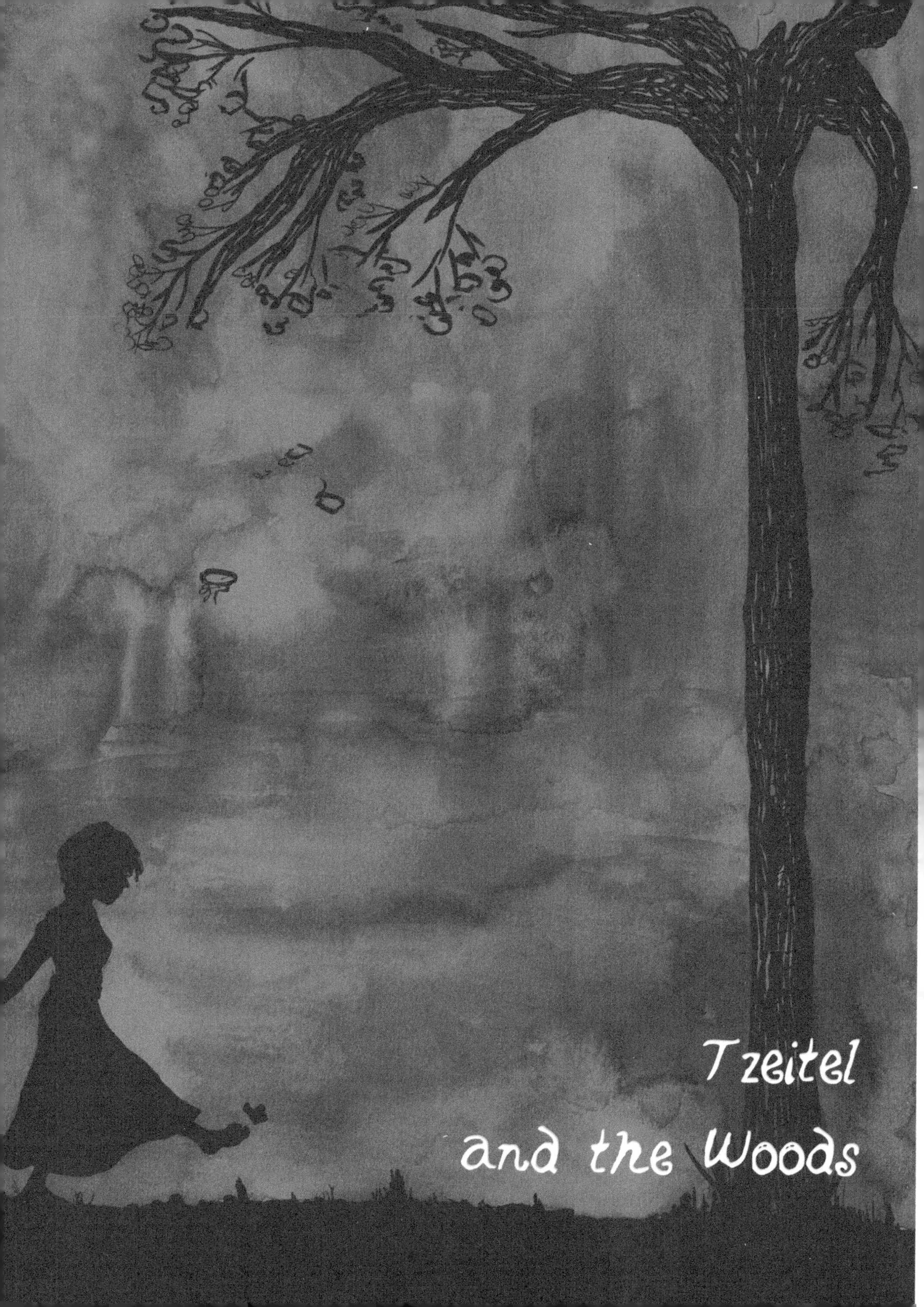
Tzeitel
and the Woods

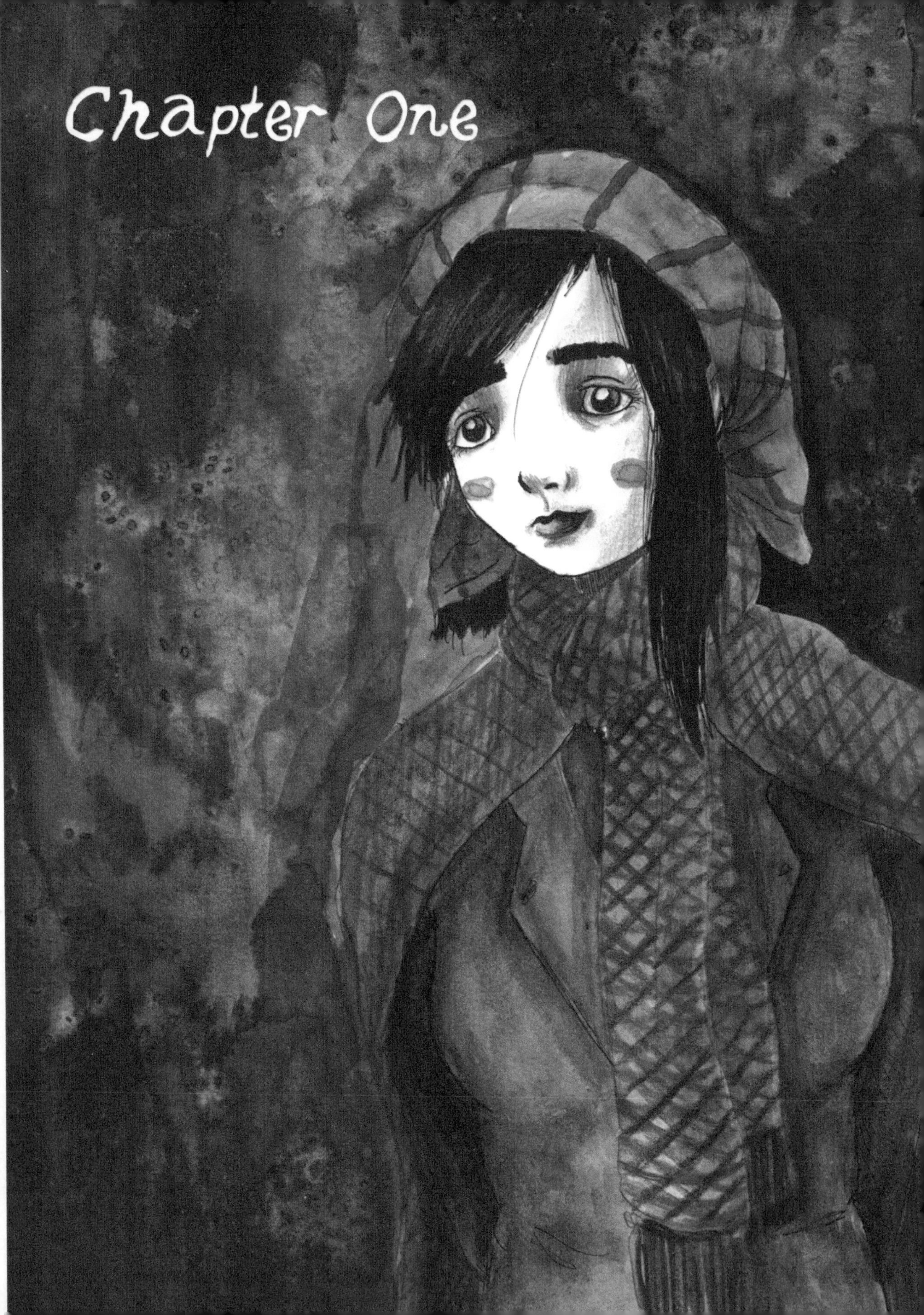
Chapter One

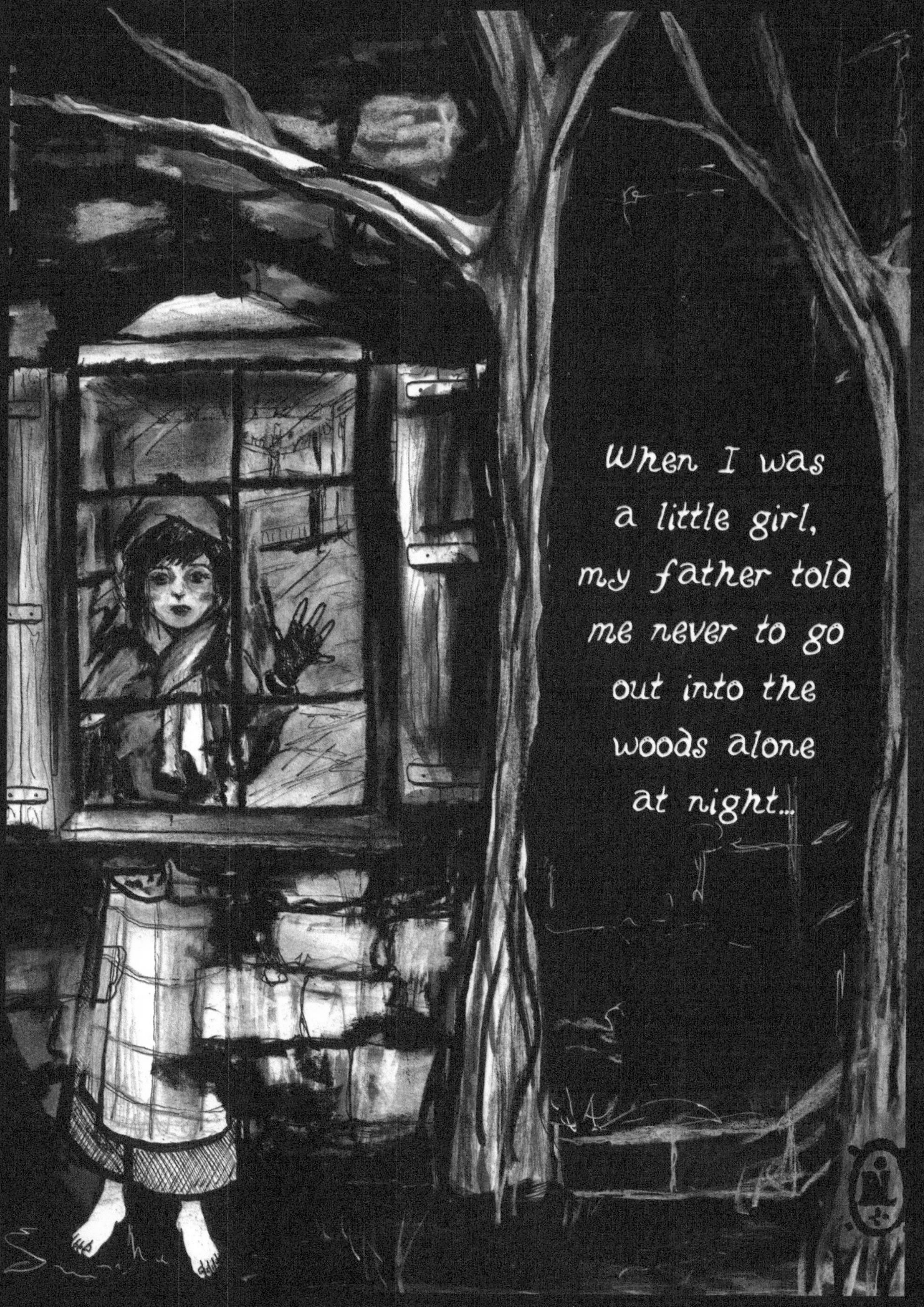
When I was
a little girl,
my father told
me never to go
out into the
woods alone
at night...

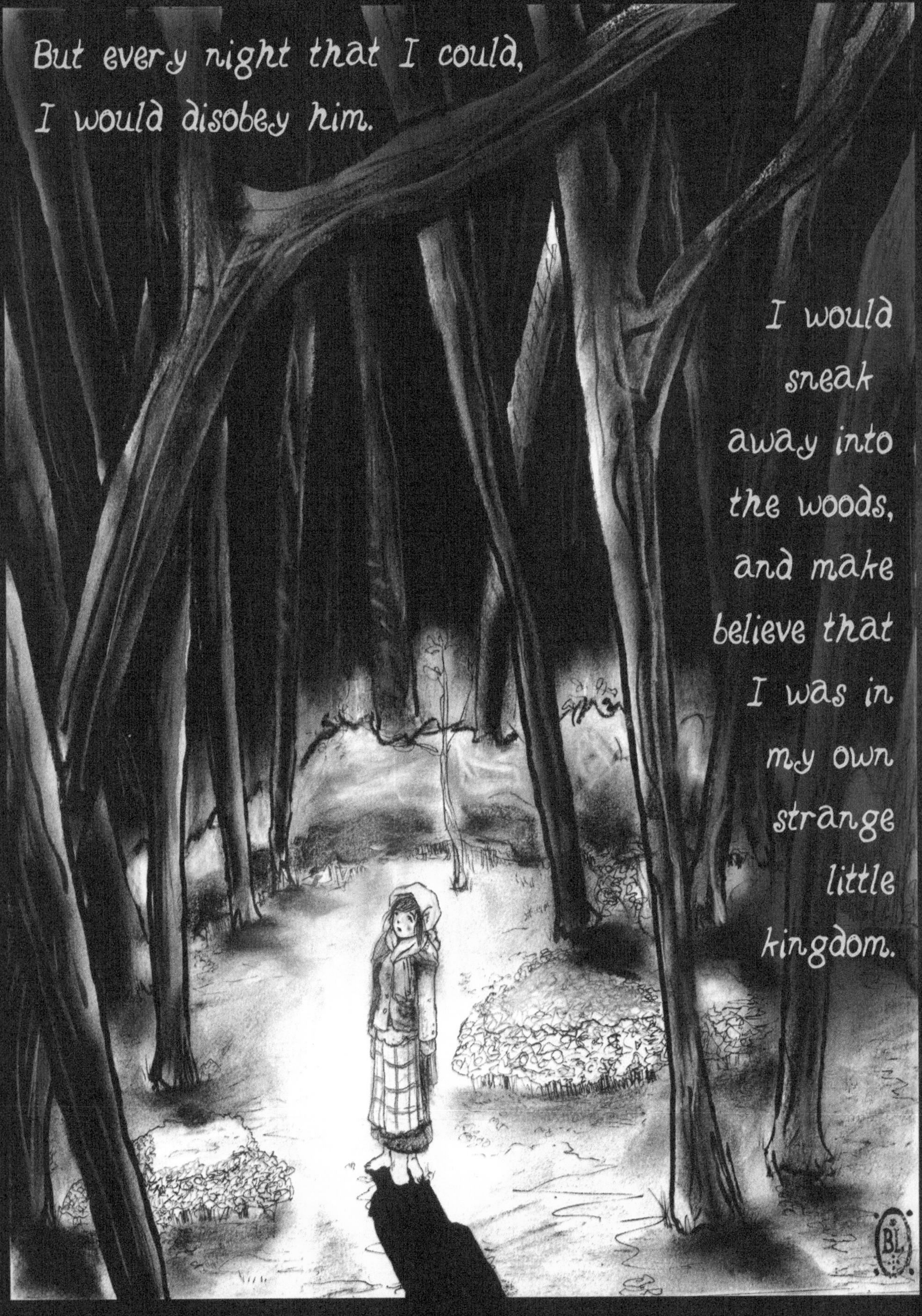
But every night that I could, I would disobey him.
I would sneak away into the woods, and make believe that I was in my own strange little kingdom.
BL

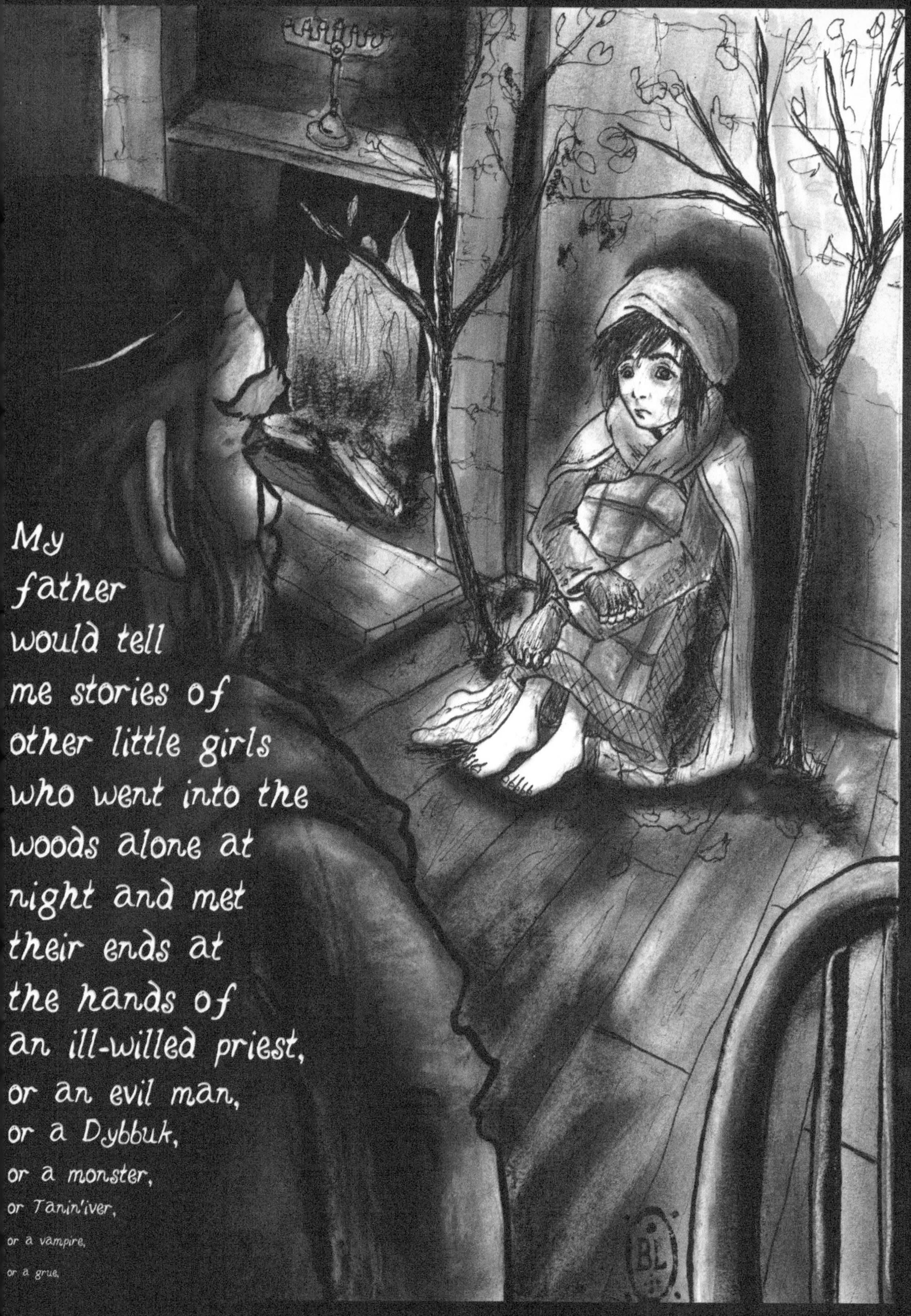
My
father
would tell
me stories of
other little girls
who went into the
woods alone at
night and met
their ends at
the hands of
an ill-willed priest,
or an evil man,
or a Dybbuk,
or a monster,
or Tanin'iver,
or a vampire,
or a grue,
BL

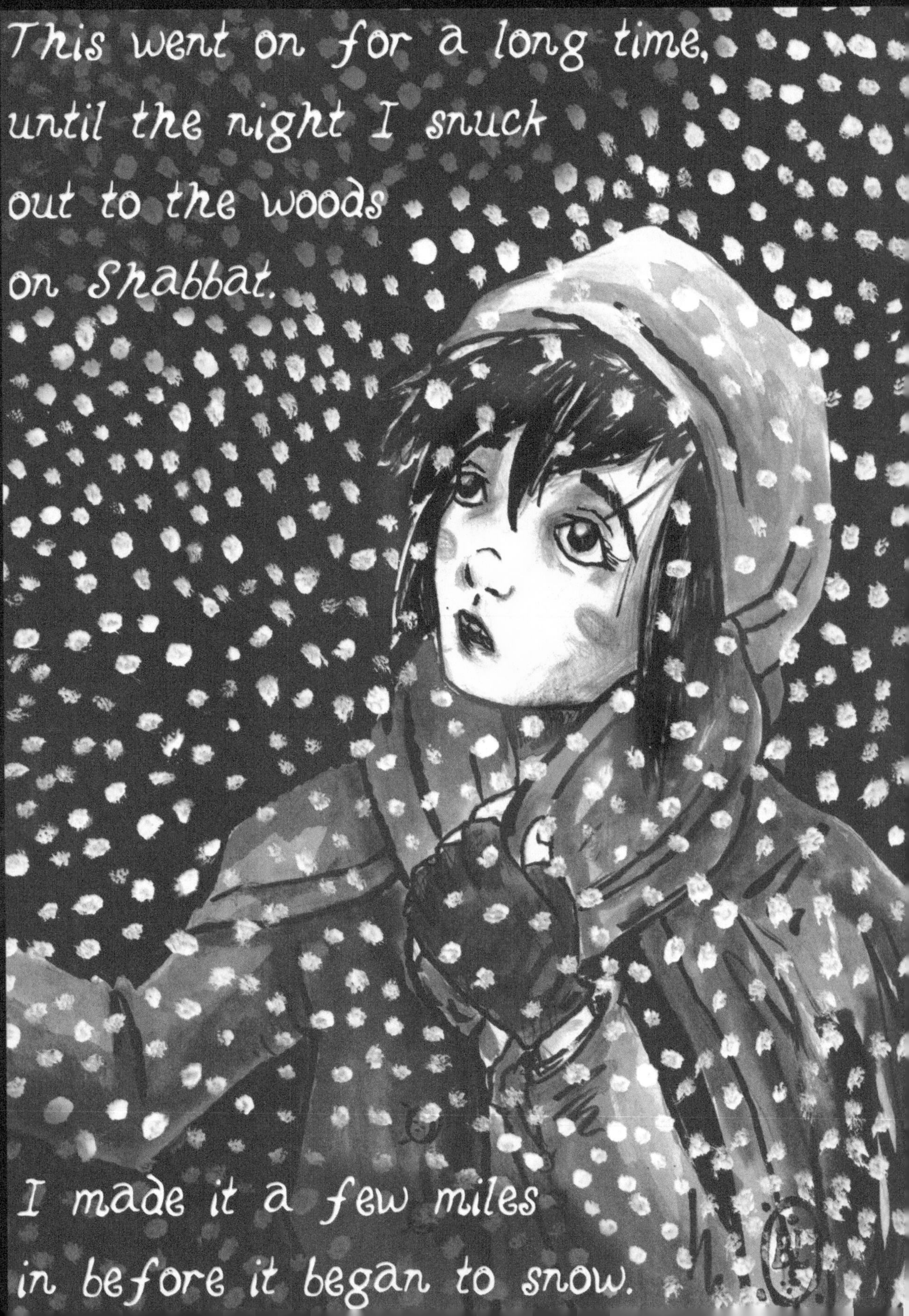
This went on for a long time, until the night I snuck out to the woods on Shabbat.
I made it a few miles in before it began to snow.

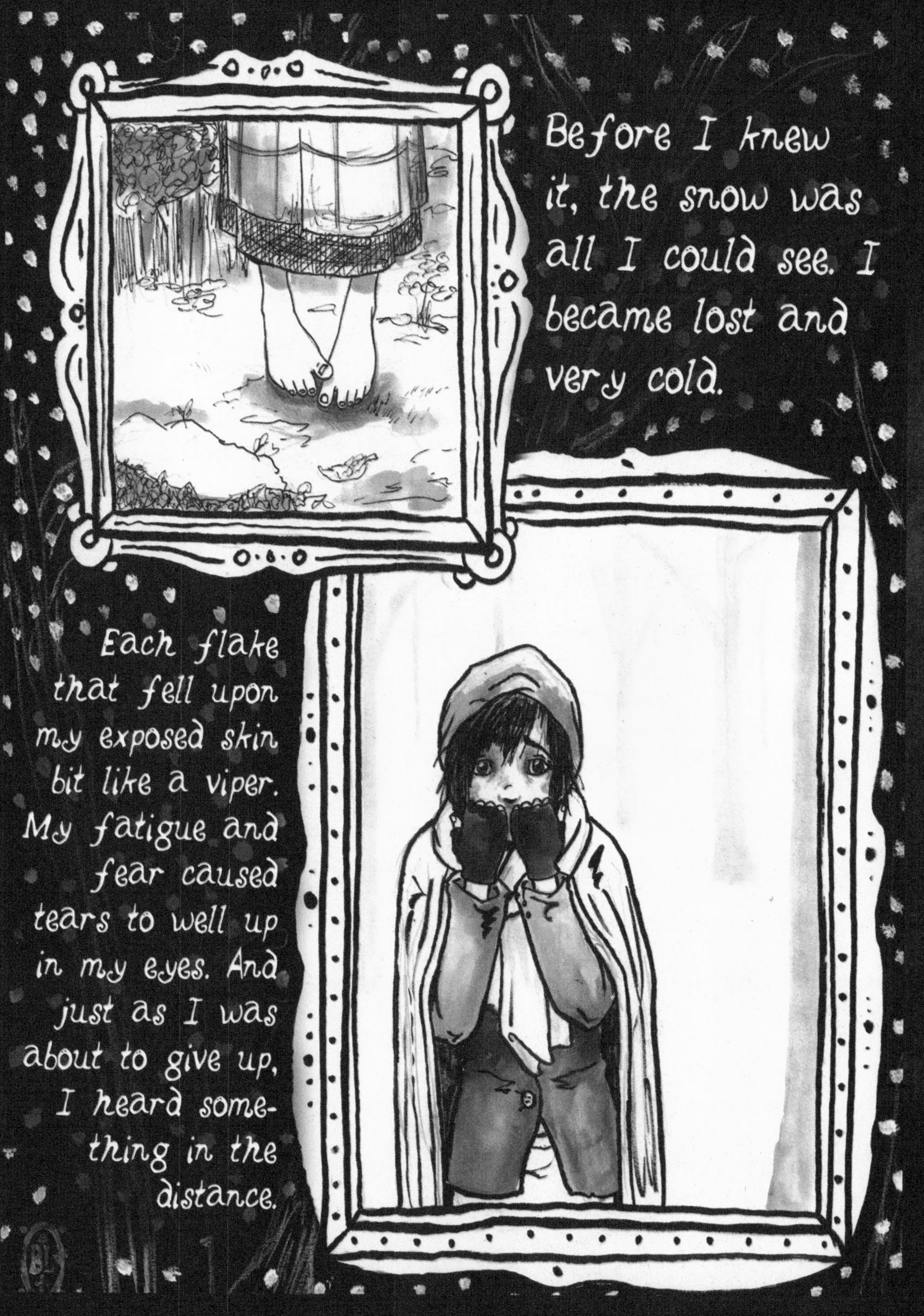
Before I knew it, the snow was all I could see. I became lost and very cold.
Each flake that fell upon my exposed skin bit like a viper. My fatigue and fear caused tears to well up in my eyes. And just as I was about to give up, I heard some-thing in the distance.

What I heard was a bellowing, yet solemn, voice.
Sh'ma Yis'ra'eil Adonai Eloheinu Adonai echad

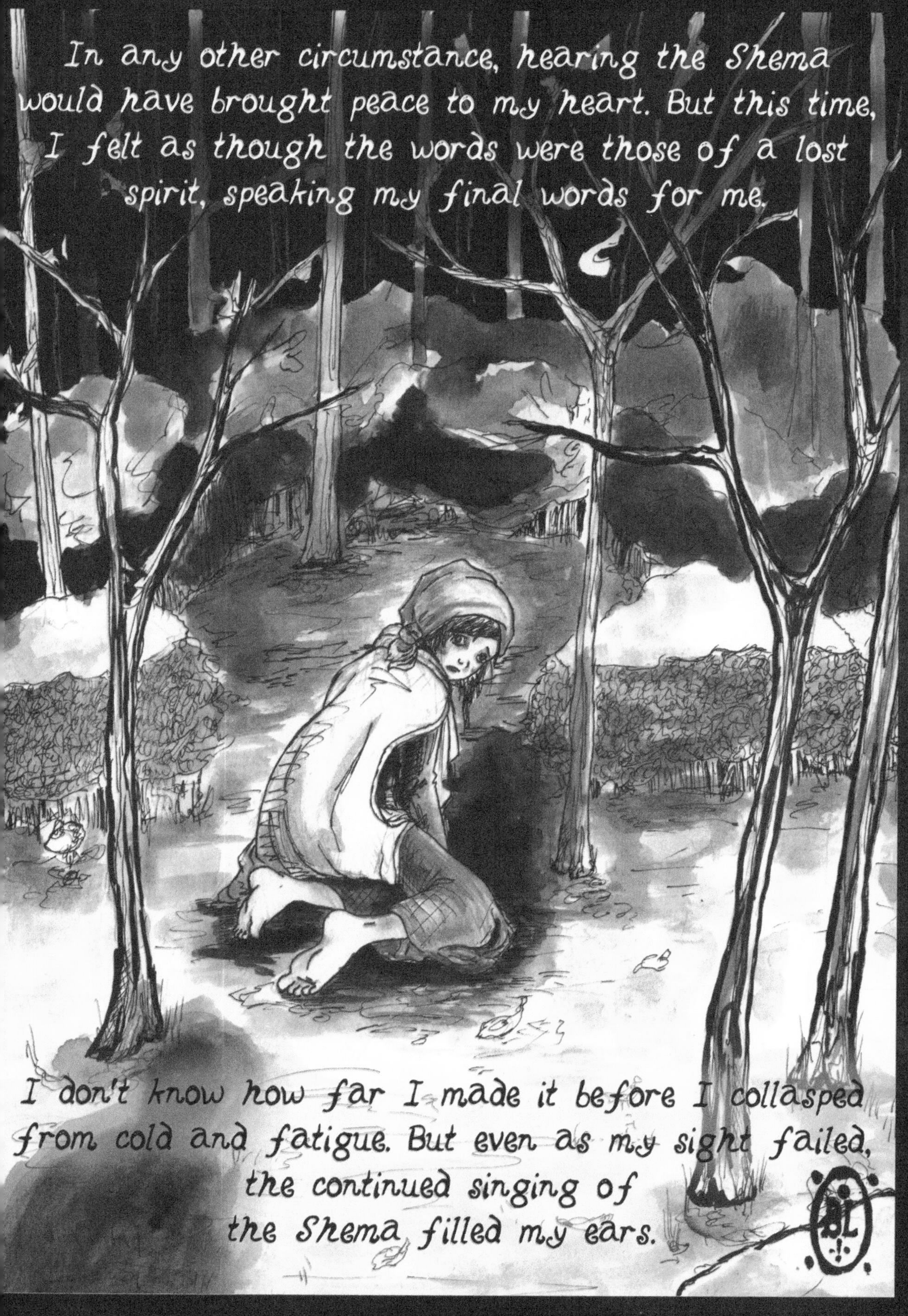
In any other circumstance, hearing the Shema would have brought peace to my heart. But this time, I felt as though the words were those of a lost spirit, speaking my final words for me.
I don't know how far I made it before I collasped from cold and fatigue. But even as my sight failed, the continued singing of the Shema filled my ears.

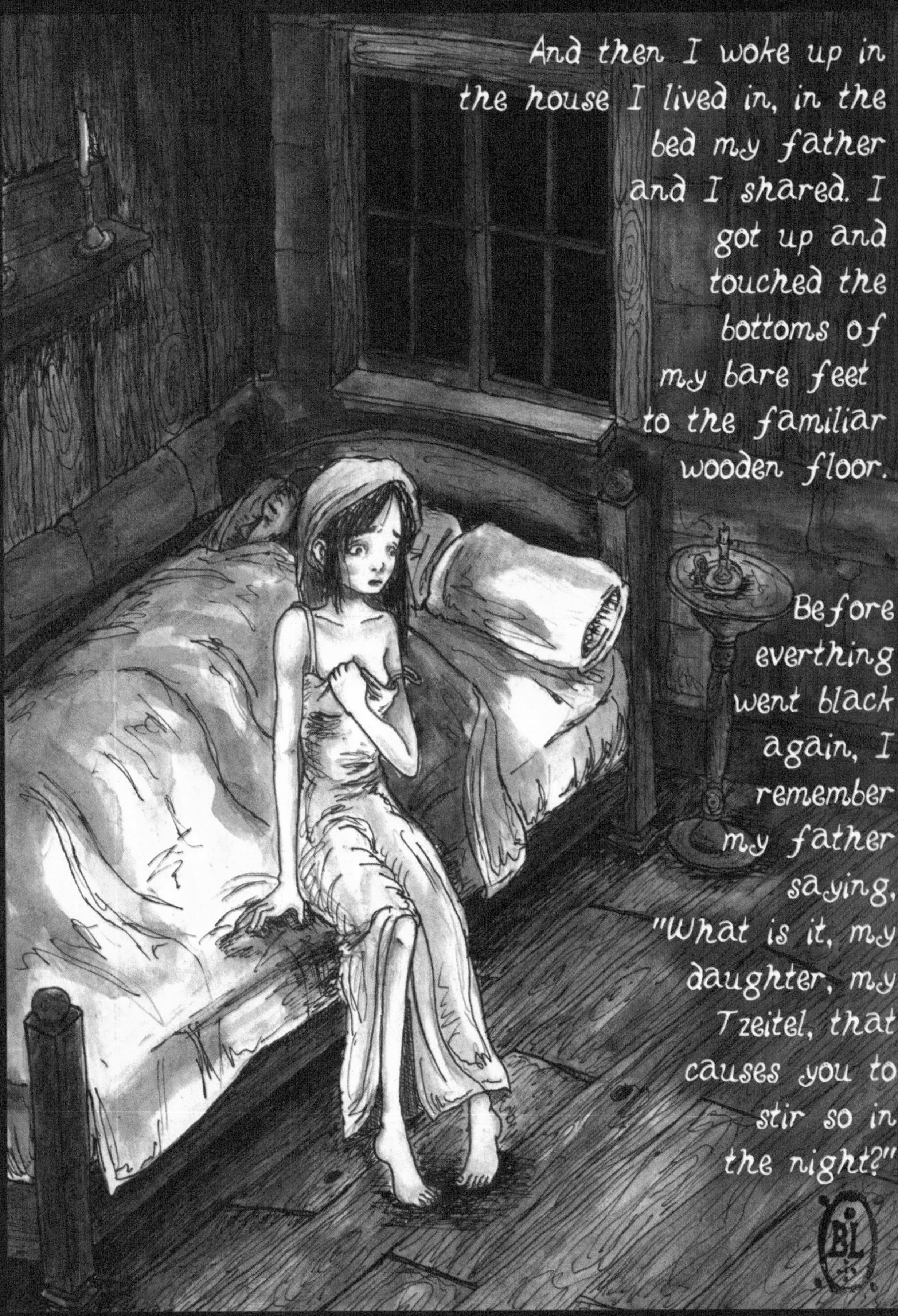
And then I woke up in the house I lived in, in the bed my father and I shared. I got up and touched the bottoms of my bare feet to the familiar wooden floor.
Before everthing went black again, I remember my father saying, "What is it, my daughter, my Tzeitel, that causes you to stir so in the night?"

My sight returned and I found myself in a cave on a thin bed of straw. A fire blazed beside me, heating my previously chilled bones. I knew this place was not part of another dream when a familiar voiced filled the lonely caverns:

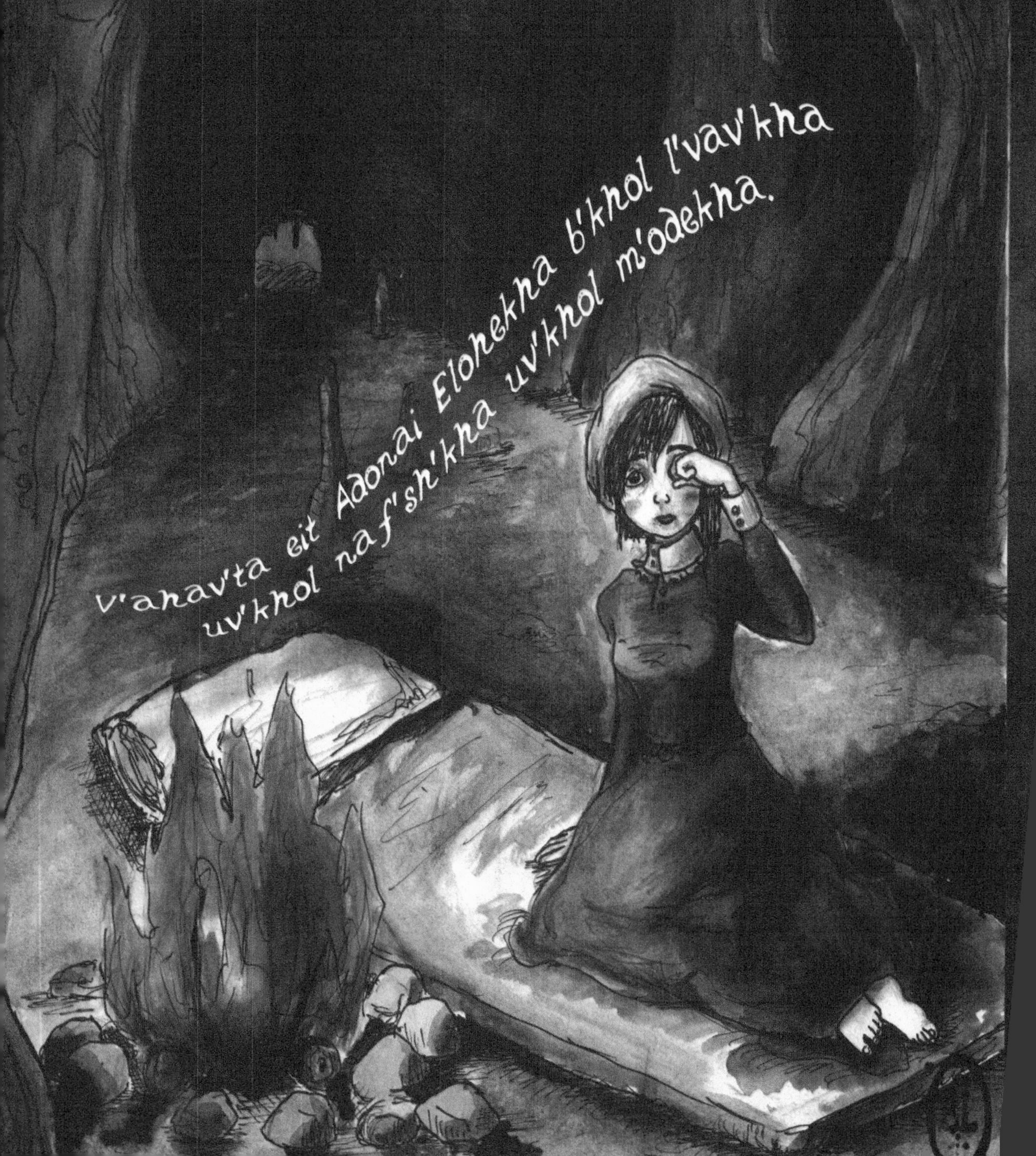
V'ahav'ta eit Adonai Elohekha b'khol l'vav'kha
uv'khol naf'sh'kha uv'khol m'odekha.

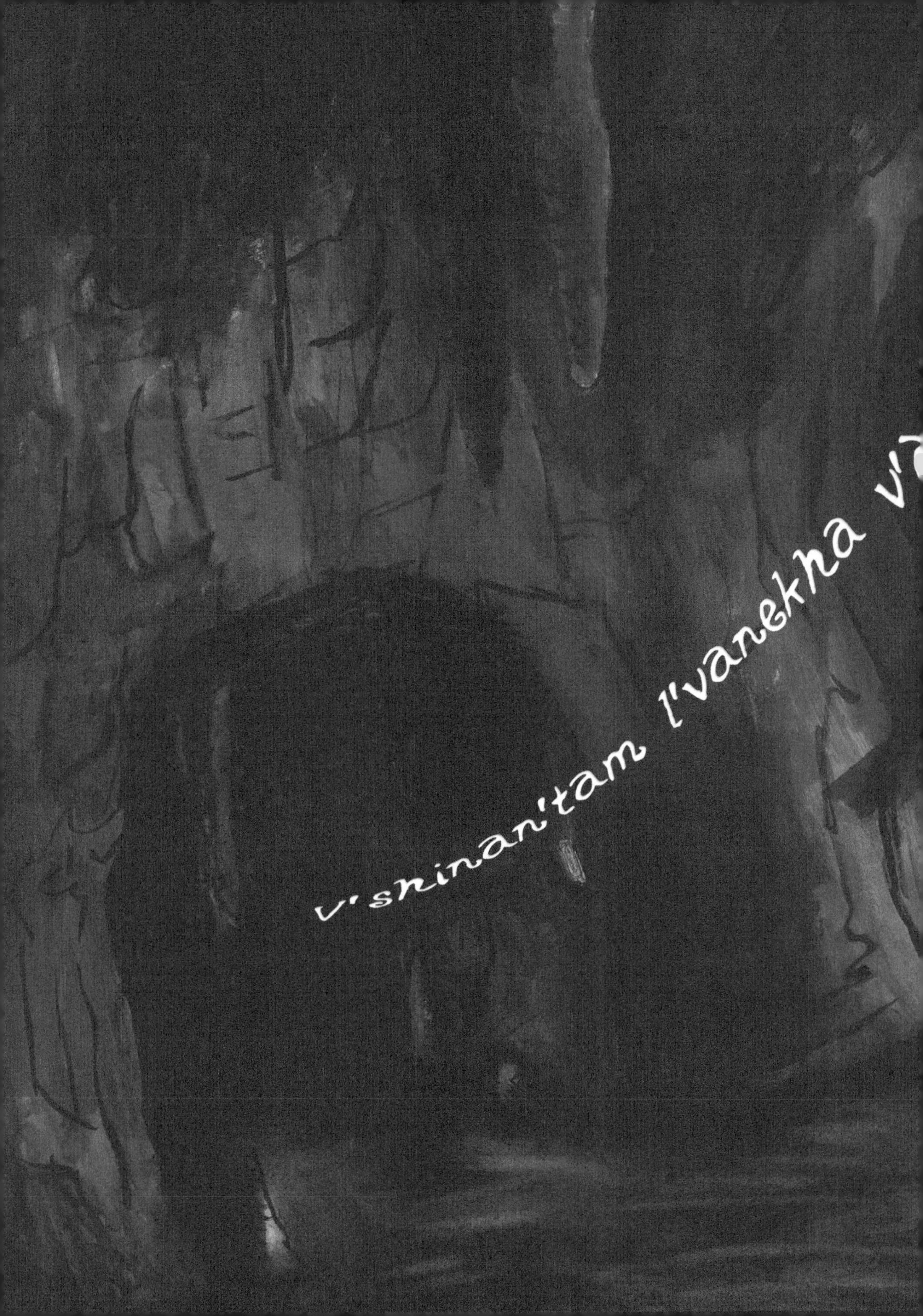
v'shinan'tam l'vanekha v'

ta bam

This time the words which filled my ears caused me no fear. As I listened closely, I could feel loneliness and despair clenching onto each syllable. I rose from the bed and followed them deeper into the cave.

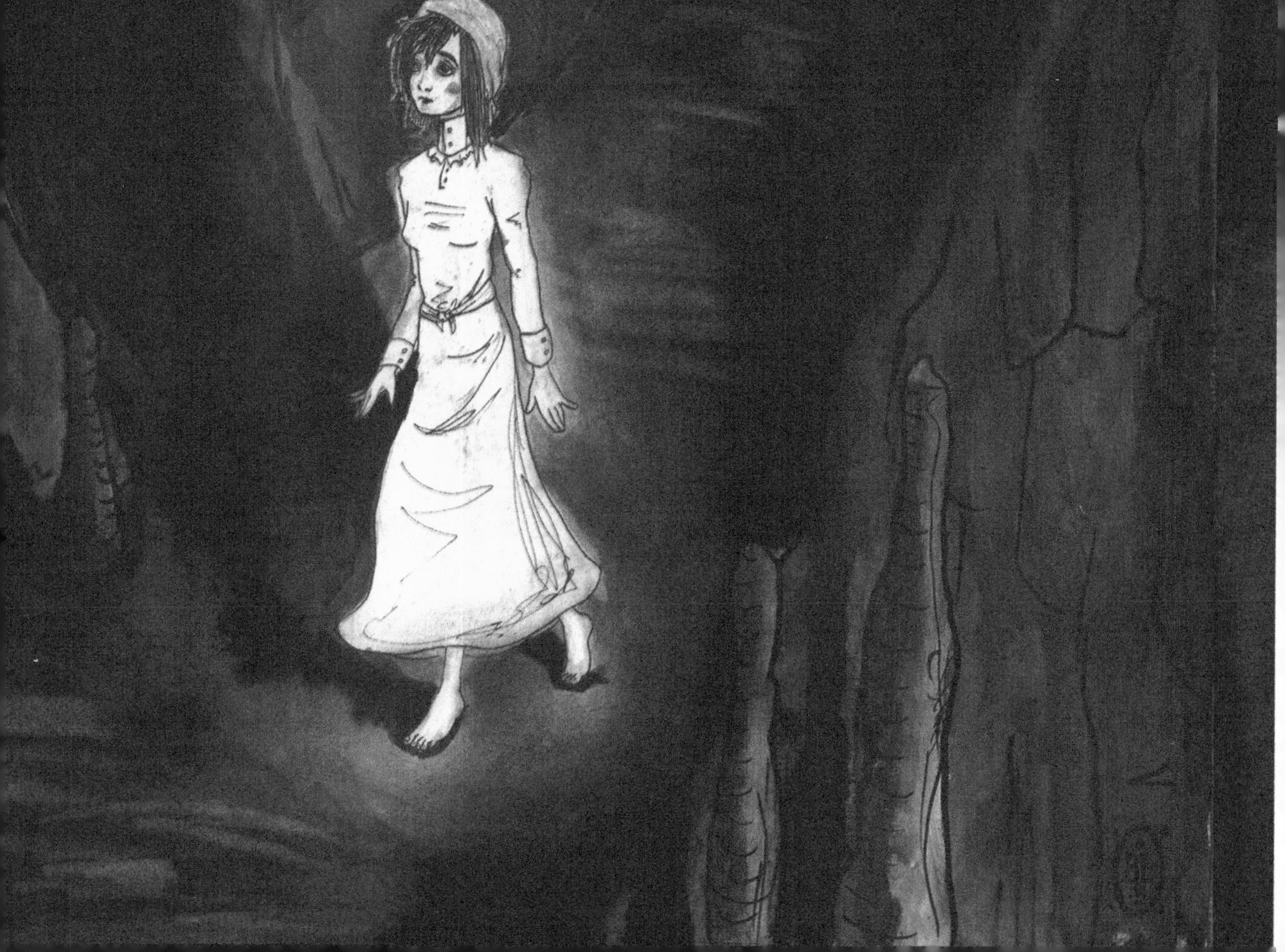

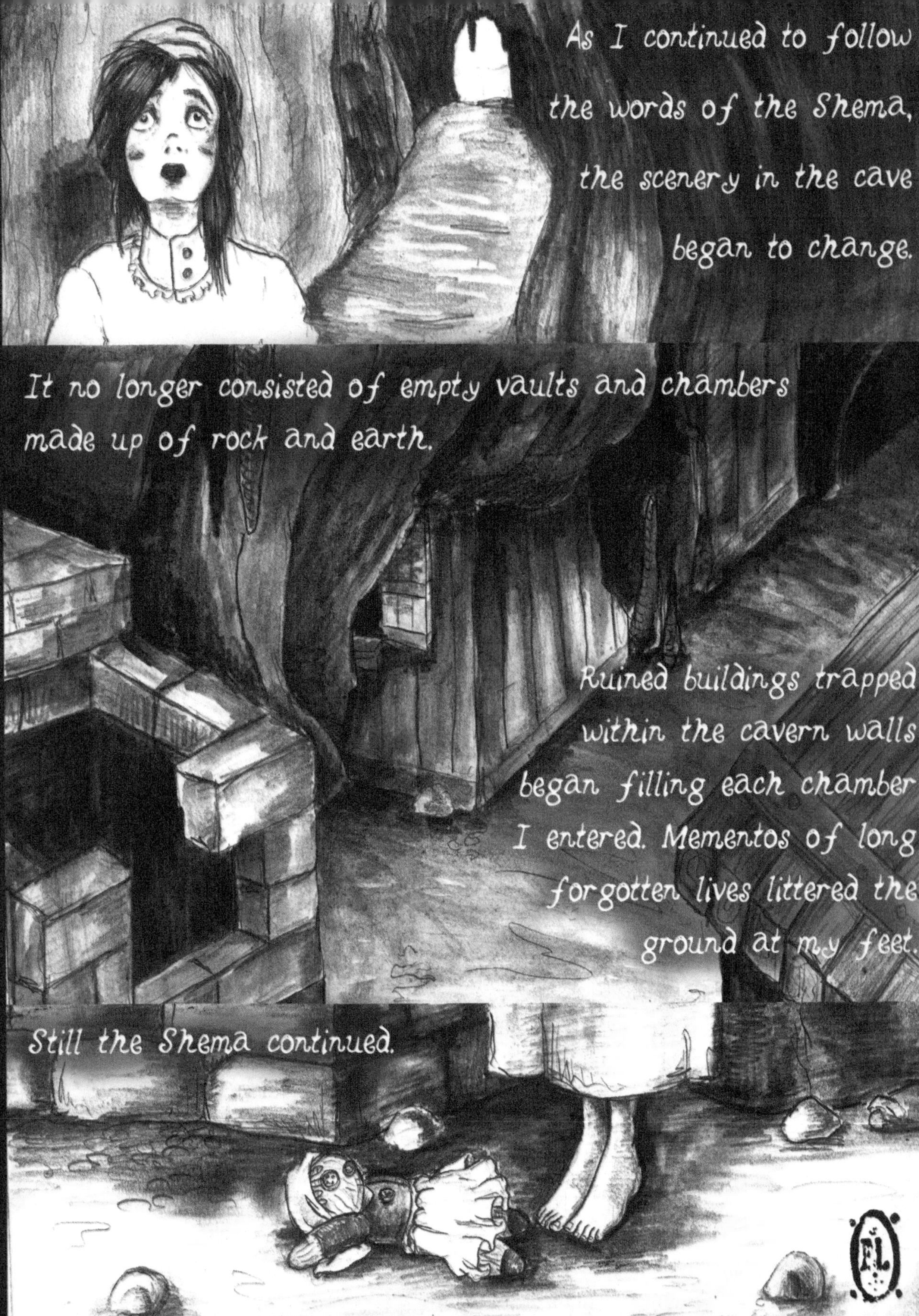
As I continued to follow the words of the Shema, the scenery in the cave began to change.
It no longer consisted of empty vaults and chambers made up of rock and earth.
Ruined buildings trapped within the cavern walls began filling each chamber I entered. Mementos of long forgotten lives littered the ground at my feet.
Still the Shema continued.

And then it ended and began again.

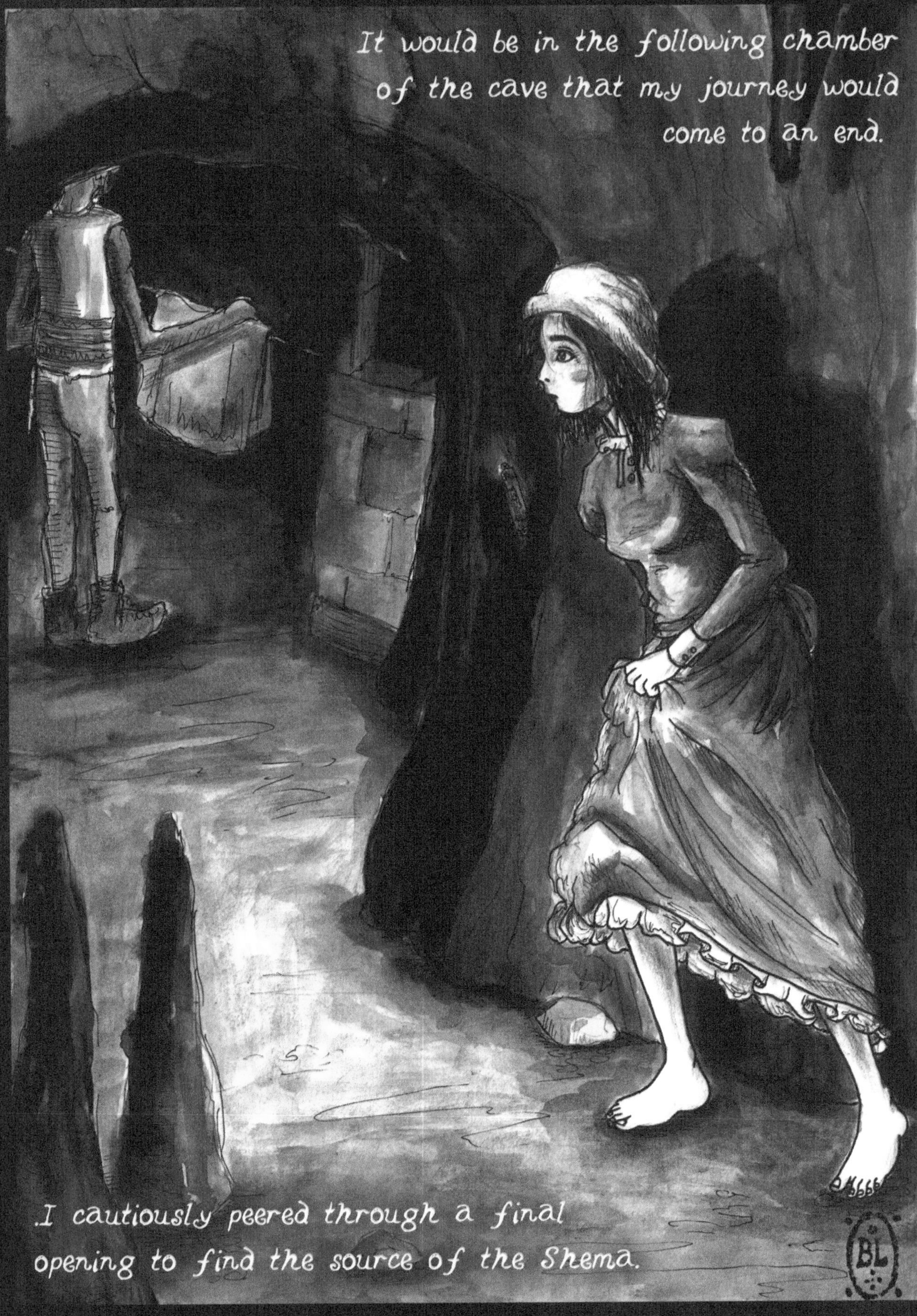
It would be in the following chamber of the cave that my journey would come to an end.
I cautiously peered through a final opening to find the source of the Shema.
BL

Chapter Two

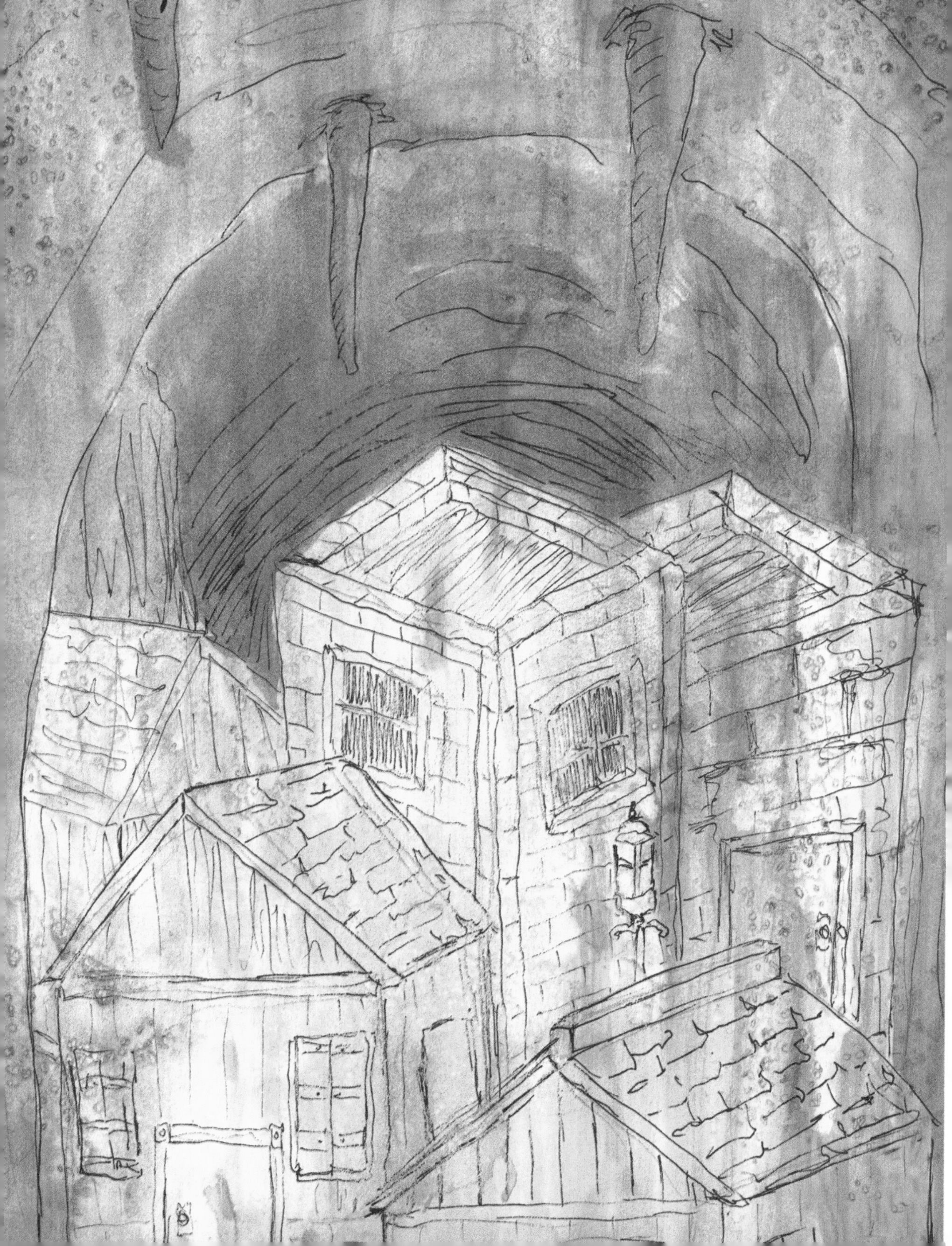

And so begins the story of Tzeitel and the Woods as she would tell it. Of course, she would have probably given it a different title. I am not here to insinuate that she wouldn't tell it correctly, or anything of the sort. I am here to refresh the parts that she cannot convey, due to all those things that time brings. I should know.

I am, however, going to take the liberty of beginning this tale a little differently. My version's beginning will end in the same way that hers will, where she discovers the source of the Shema, as it will end in the same way once the last pages of this book are turned. The change between the two, however, will be concerned with the very beginning. I would like to start a little earlier.

Tzeitel, who was becoming more and more of a young woman and less of a child by the day, lived in a forest alone with her father. They inhabited a small cottage that was maintained only within approximation. The nearest village was a day's walk by way of foot. She never understood why they had left the village, which is where they lived up until a few years ago. She assumed for a long time that their regular visitors had stopped coming because they had perhaps forgotten the way. The cottage had been built some distance within the boundaries of the forest and any merchants or friends who would visit would complain. Complaints were about all Tzeitel heard of the conversations these people had with her father when they arrived. Her father never told her what they were about, and after she grew up, she was thankful. They were the kinds of words that make children grow up too quickly.

It was probably because her father had been so tight lipped with her that she began to disobey him. Of all the laws he laid before her, which on the whole weren't so bad, not going into the forest at night was the most important. This of course, as you have just read, was the one thing Tzeitel truly enjoyed. Life was not easy for either of them in their new home, but that is not to say that their lives were particularly comfortable before.

Tzeitel was born the only daughter to a brush maker and his wife. The three of them lived in ravaging poverty. When Tzeitel's mother became ill, life became harder when more money was needed for a doctor, and when she died, there was no one to take care of little Tzeitel except her father. Had her father not made the decision for them to leave the village they probably would have lost their house to the local government anyway. This way, their house had put a little money for goods into their pockets. But no matter how great a feeling of security the preparedness for a journey can give you, it is never enough to combat the sadness from having to leave in the first place. Nor does it cure the homesickness you feel afterwards, especially if you have no choice in the matter. Tzeitel had no choice in the matter, but independently from her, despite the fact he made the choice, her father felt the same way.

Each year provided new difficulties for Tzeitel and her father and Tzeitel eventually found herself trying to escape them. She would have never thought of leaving her father alone, so instead her head rose into the clouds, and she spent every minute she could in the forest. It was her longing for a different life that got her in the position that it did. But it is always that initial dream that sets growth and discovery into motion.

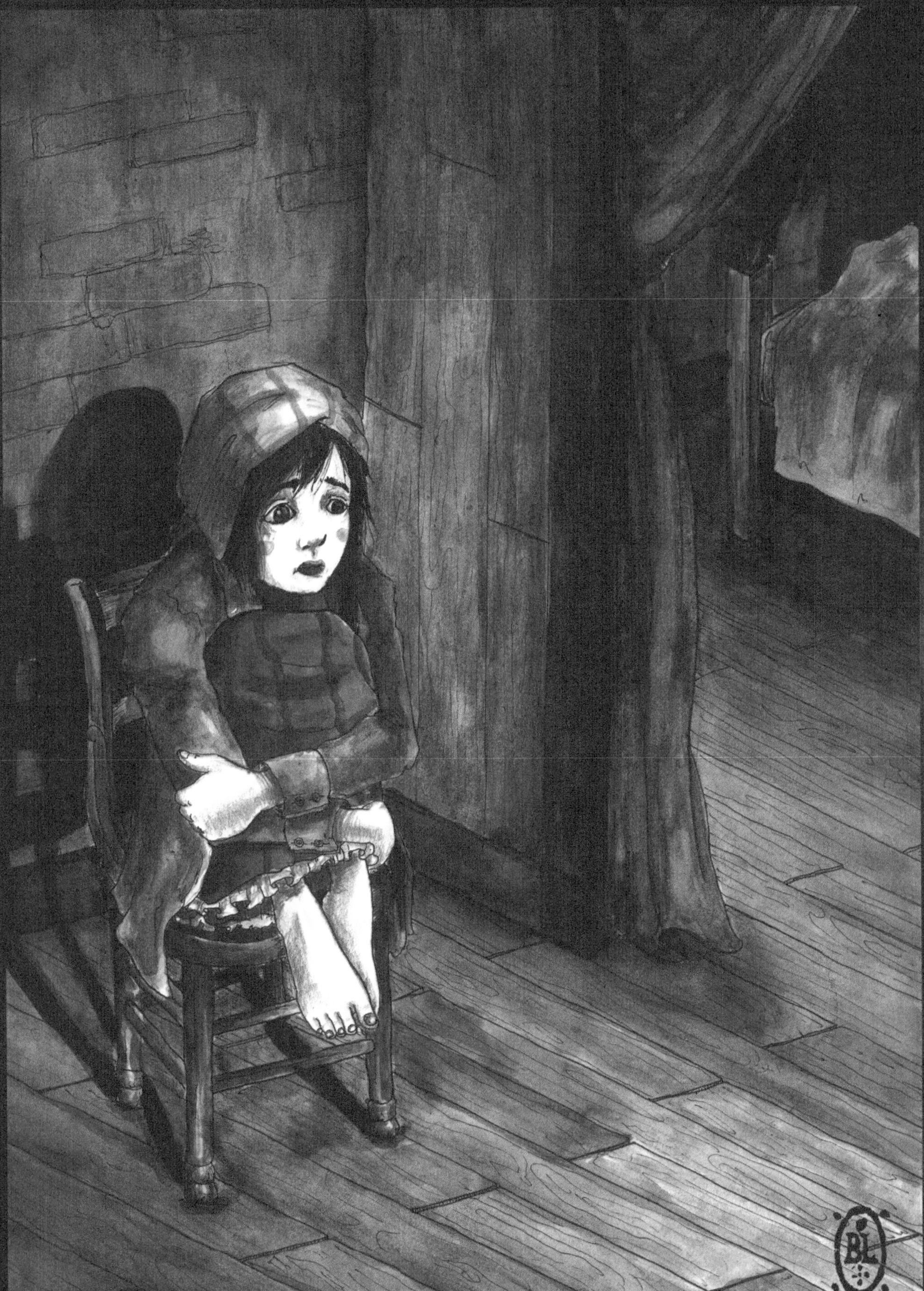

And here our Tzeitel is: what she was about to discover would irrevocably change her life. Within the next chamber of the cave, as her tiny feet carried her therein, she saw a towering figure leaning over a line between two crumbling houses. It busied itself with the care of her winter clothes, which had become soaked from her time lying in the snow.

She continued her advance as the figure uttered the words of the Shema in its low, yet timid sing-song voice. Hearing it up close like this filled her with a sense of immense reverence, but such solemnness gave way for the sadness behind the words to be revealed. She tip toed further into the chamber and closer to this creature which had obviously saved her life. Even though she felt no fear, her face was filled with an awe that suggested otherwise.

As she further advanced, the creature's prayer came to an end and it began again. Tzeitel paid even closer attention to the words and began to wonder why this strange being sounded as though it was in such despair. At first she wondered if it mourned the death of a friend or a lover. Had it lost its family a long time ago? Or had it done some terrible thing that it now regrets? Whatever the case may have been, the curious girl could do nothing to stop imagining entire back stories for the thing. By the time she stood next to it she had considered every possible fact about it save that it could be dangerous.

The creature, which seemed to be loosely based on the form of a human male, stood at nearly two times her own height. She rose to the tips of her toes and cocked her head as far back as she could manage to get a look at its face. She was not certain if it was ignoring her, or was genuinely unaware of her presence. For throughout the entire distance that had she covered, it had continued on with its recitation of the old prayer and did not stop when she arrived. Tzeitel, who was a bit more nervous standing next to it, finally gathered up her nerve and reached out for one of its tzitzits, fashioned to its tallit katan. Her tiny hand gave it a good yank as though she were ringing a bell. The creature stopped signing. It turned its head and looked down at her. Tzeitel bit her lower lip and curled her toes hard into the cavern floor.

"Excuse me," she began in a shaky voice, "but what are you?"

The creature stopped singing and did not speak for a long time and Tzeitel wondered if it could understand her. Just as she was about to rephrase her query, the thing answered.

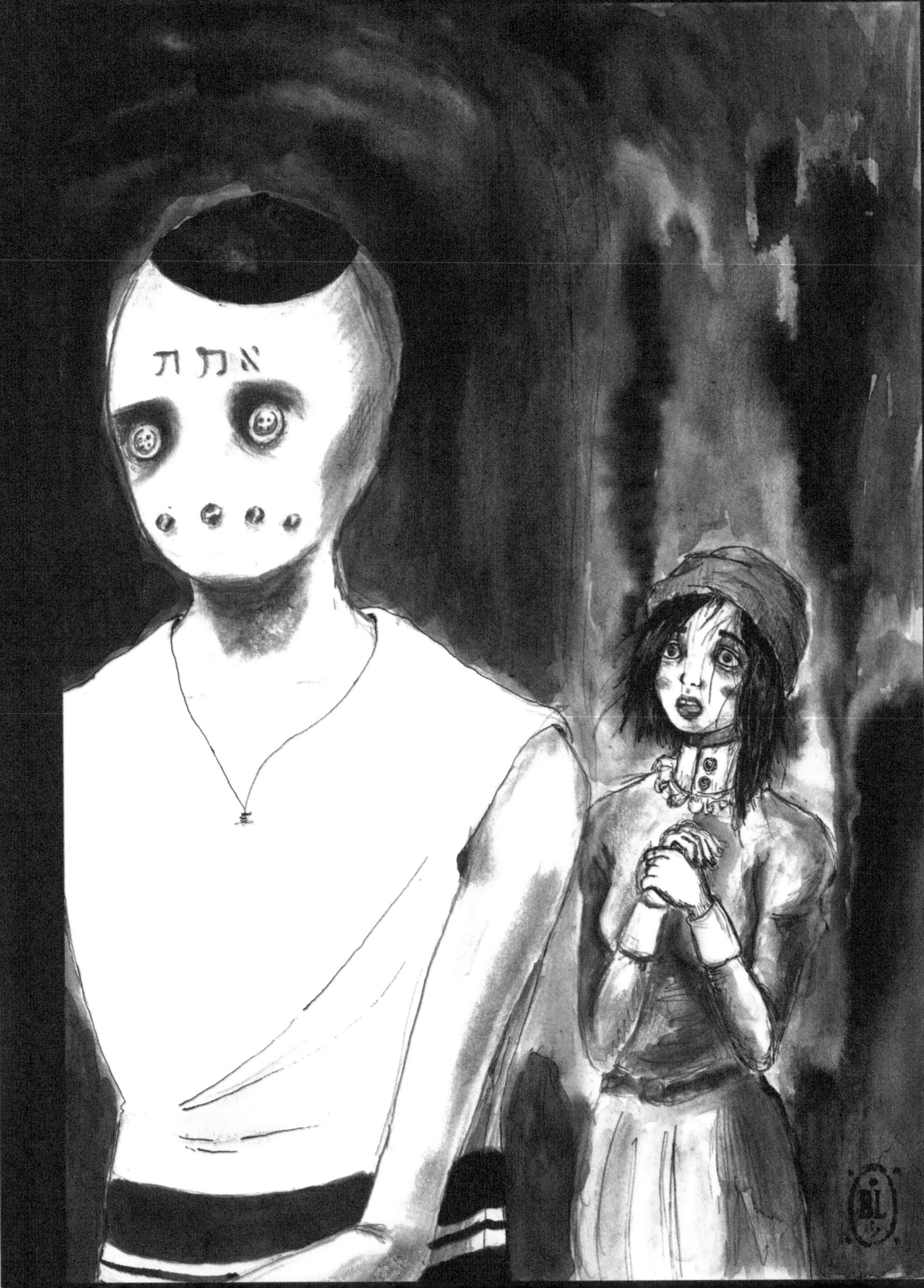
אמת

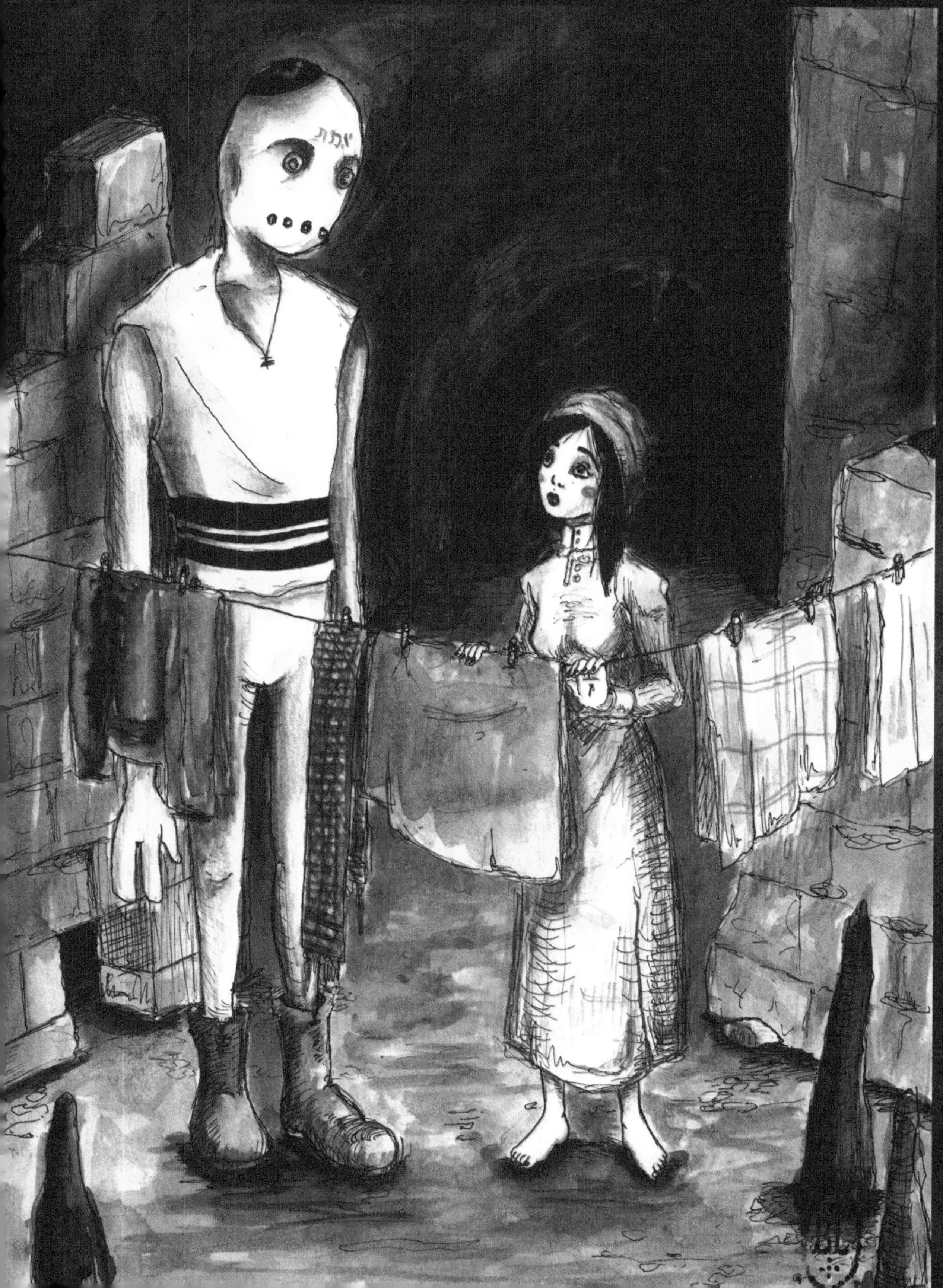
אמת

"What I am is not important," it said in a slow midrange voice. "What is important is that you are alive and safe from harm."

With that it returned its attention to the girl's laundry and began singing the Shema again from the beginning.

Tzeitel was not sure how to proceed after hearing the answer she was given, should one be so flexible as to call such a response an answer. In the end, she decided to move on and, once again, gave the monster's tzitzit another ring. As it had done previously, it stopped its prayer and mechanically diverted its attention to her.

"Pardon me," the curious youth began again, "but why do you keep singing the Shema over and over again?"

This pause in dialogue was a shorter one. "Because, little one, I am dying," the creature said. "Now if you please, I would greatly appreciate no further interruptions. I do not have a lot of time and I can utter no other words than those of the Shema."

The creature began from the beginning yet another time and left Tzeitel to her own thoughts. Tzeitel's initial reaction was one of disappointment that the creature seemed reluctant to speak with her. Then came pity—pity that the creature was dying. Then, after some time more, came doubt. It seemed to Tzeitel that such a statement made little sense if the events surrounding her arrival to this cave were examined.

This creature was obviously her savior: it was what had rescued her from freezing to death in the forest. However, its statement made little sense because if it were really dying, what was it doing out in a blizzard? Would it have been able to carry her back to the cave with it? And does a dying person really spend their time hanging that evening's laundry (on Shabbat of all days)? She remembered hearing the Shema in the woods and that meant that, if the creature had not stopped (of which she had no doubts), it would have been saying it this entire time. She did not know how long she had lain unconscious in the snow, or how long she had slept before waking in the cave. She wondered if indeed the creature really was dying, did it really have all this time to recite the Shema as many times as it must have had done. She scrunched up her tiny face and gave one of the creature's tzitzits a demanding tug.

"Are you sure that you're really dying?" she asked as it turned its head towards her.

"Oh, yes. You see, the aleph inscribed upon my forehead is fading." The creature raised a giant hand and pointed to the spot. "I have failed G-d, and because of this failure G-d is slowly turning me off."

Tzeitel got back up on her tip toes and strained to see the word emet, which was lightly carved into the creature's forehead. As far as she could tell, it looked perfectly legible as though it had been chiseled in the morning before.

"It doesn't look like its fading to me," she said sheepishly.

The creature frowned and turned away from her. In a voice which only feigned irritation it said, "Please, I must return to the Shema."

But Tzeitel didn't give the creature a chance to continue.

"You know," she said, "I'm dying too."

With this the creature turned to her in a somewhat manner of shock.

"Oh, yes," the girl went on, noticing this. "Every day brings a person closer to their deaths. A person can die at any time for whatever reason. But with that in mind, how could I expect to get anything done in life if all I did was sing the Shema because I was afraid that I wouldn't say it at the right time?"

The creature did not say anything.

"Please do not think of me as rude," the girl continued, "but I would think someone who just saved the life of a young girl would understand that."

The creature turned away from her and said nothing for a long time. It should be noted that that silence included the Shema.

"Your words are older than you are, little one," the creature muttered whimsically. "What you do not understand is that I have failed G-d, as I have said. My life consists only of my failure, and it is that failure that defines G-d's sight of me. I live my winter years, not in the exile of my home, but of my spirit."

"How did you fail G-d?" Tzeitel asked with sincere concern.

"I do not remember."

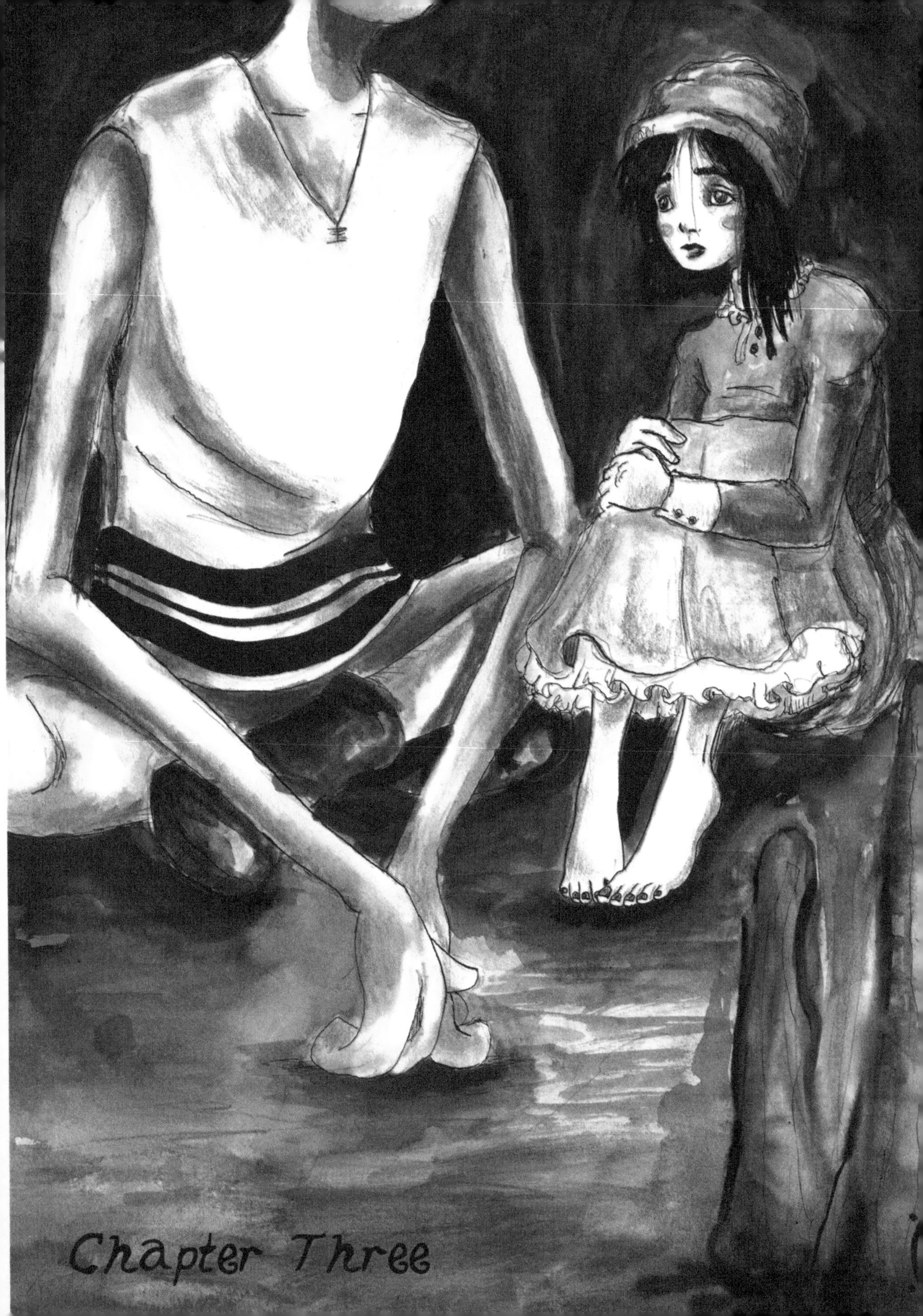
Chapter Three

The conversation which ensued was a long one. It was one where Tzeitel cleverly led the unwitting creature away from her clothes hanging on the line, and to a more comfortable spot. Within an old building Tzeitel found a weathered and ancient bed in which to sit, across from a nice spot on the open floor that the creature decided to occupy.

In the time it took for the two to find their way to their new environment, Tzeitel had been able to convince the creature to stop singing the Shema more than necessary. Although she probably could not have cited this as the cause at the time, the creature's cessation of the prayer was more likely due to the simple fact it had someone to talk to. And Tzeitel, unaware of her own desire for companionship, soon became just as lost in the good company. This is what caused the two of them to talk even deeper into the night and through the morning. Tzeitel would eventually fall asleep and wake up the following day. But I mustn't get ahead of myself; much has to be covered before the story can move on.

Tzeitel was surprised to find out that the creature was a golem. Although in retrospect she found it strange that with her imagination, and love of fairy tales, she failed to recognize it sooner. Golems were very much alive in the folklore of her old Rabbi and her father. Although this answer to her first question did not please her as one might imagine. Along with the recollected tales, came the ones where the golems eventually go mad and turn on their creators. This disquieting notion was short lived; however, as she found the golem to be shy, pleasantly awkward, and at times a little slow-witted. Along with these qualities, the golem was quite friendly after it began warming up to her.

The golem had no name, although it remembered being called many things. It did not remember who made it or for what purpose. Along with vague details and foggy inclinations, a town was all it could recall. Tzeitel wondered if it was like trying to remember a wonderful dream that you instantly forget upon waking. It could not say why it no longer lived in the town or what happened to it, and she wondered if the place they were in now was, once upon a time, the very town from the golem's past. When she asked this, the golem agreed that it seemed reasonable, but was all the more upset because of its failure.

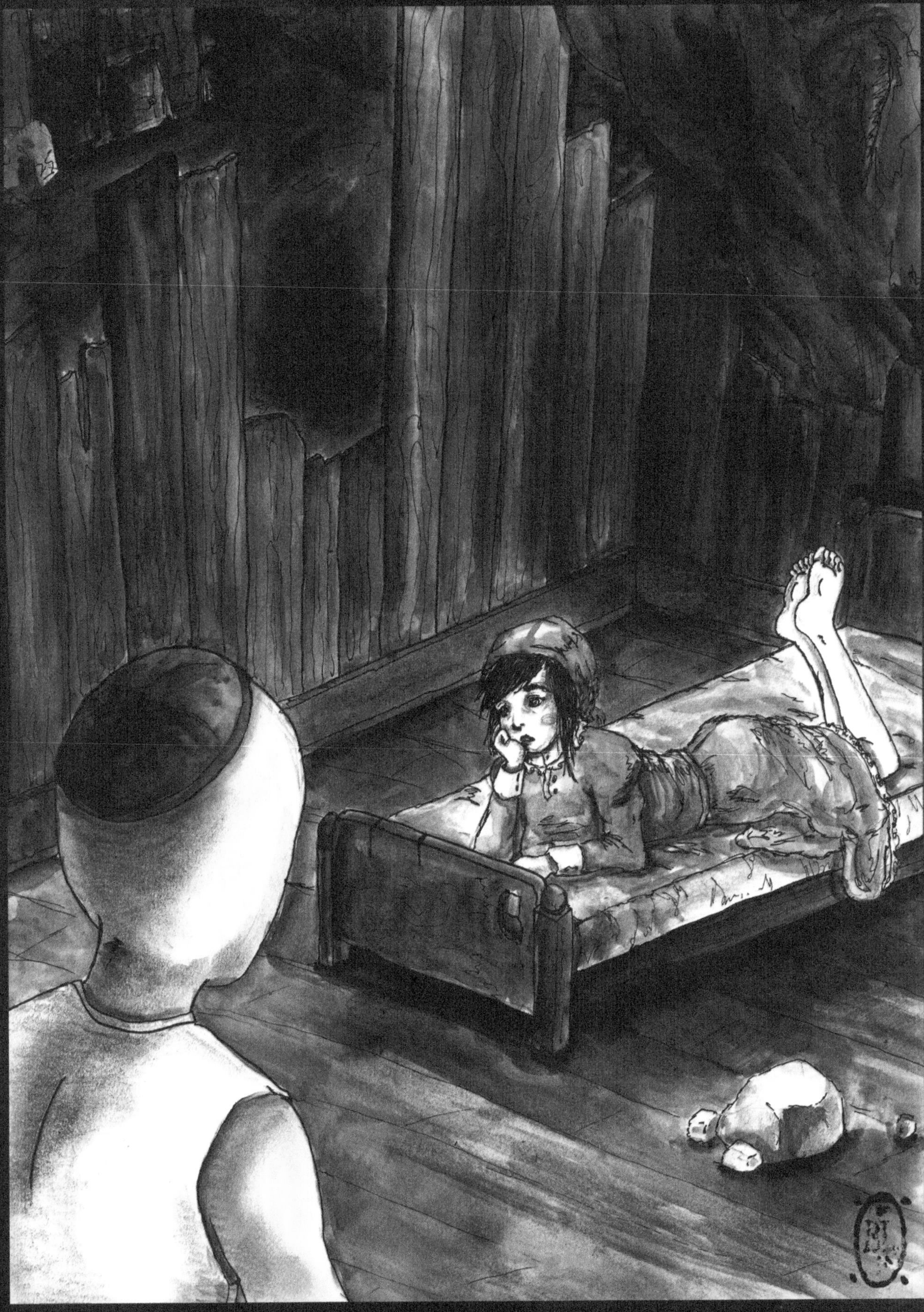

"Assuming this place used to be your home, how can you possibly think all of this is your fault?" Tzeitel demanded as her arms waved about, referencing the dilapidated constructs around them.

But unfortunate topics did not occupy the conversation for long. The golem, as it went, turned out to be just as curious about her as she was of it. Soon Tzeitel found herself fondly recounting her days living in her village, describing her father, and sharing her hopes and dreams. But this peaceful time did not last long. It seemed that all of these topics were interrelated, and that relationship was based in her recount of her old village. Why she dreamed of finding a different life, why her father behaved in the way he did, and how they found themselves living alone in a remote forest. It was at that point Tzeitel recalled old stories she had heard about the goyim attacking Jews, and suddenly, the scenery in the cave became all too familiar. She didn't want to believe it, but having years to think about it, she realized that her own life would have resembled the crumbling buildings in the cave, had her father not moved them away. A single word dangled off the bottom of her lower lip and it was by accident that she said it aloud.

"Pogrom."

"What was that?" The golem asked in a near state of fervor.

"Is this what happened to this place?" Tzeitel asked after a moment. She thought back to her journey through the cave and, although she did not notice it much at the time, she recalled having seen mezuzahs on doorways, Stars of David drawn here and there, and a variety of other objects suggesting that Jews had once lived there.

"I'm not really sure," the golem said solemnly. "I fear though that this place is in the condition it is on my account."

"What did you do?" Tzeitel asked captivated.

"I think it is more of what I did not do," was the golem's sorrowful response.

"Is that what you meant by failing G-d? Were you supposed to protect this place?"

"With the many years that I have been here, alone with my thoughts, that notion had occurred to me. Why would I, being such the thing that I am, be the only one left after all the others had gone?"

"I'm sure it wasn't your fault that this happened," Tzeitel said, curling up and wrapping her arms around her legs.

"How do you know, little one?" The golem asked.

"How could someone like you, who would save the life of one little girl, let an entire village die? You're so kind and sensitive. I can't believe it."

The golem bowed its head and Tzeitel wondered if its button eye were capable of making tears. She slipped off the bed and went to the creature. She took as much she could of one of the golem's giant hands in both of hers. It was likely that these were the only kind words that anyone had ever said to the golem. Although Tzeitel cannot say for sure, my place is to now tell you that if it could, the golem would have cried at that point. But instead, Tzeitel cried for him. She rested her head against his massive chest and wept. All the while the golem wondered how it could be that someone who didn't even know him could be so kind. The golem took its free hand and, like a warm blanket, draped it over the tiny child's back. The two of them remained this way for some time before Tzeitel finally rose and smiled at the golem.

"Since you cannot remember your name," she said wiping away her tears, "I have thought of one for you."

The round stones that made up the golems mouth curled up into a weak smile.

"I will call you Avi," she said.

It was just then that the golem realized that it did not know Tzeitel's name.

"What are you called?" it asked.

"Tzeitel."

"It's a lovely name."

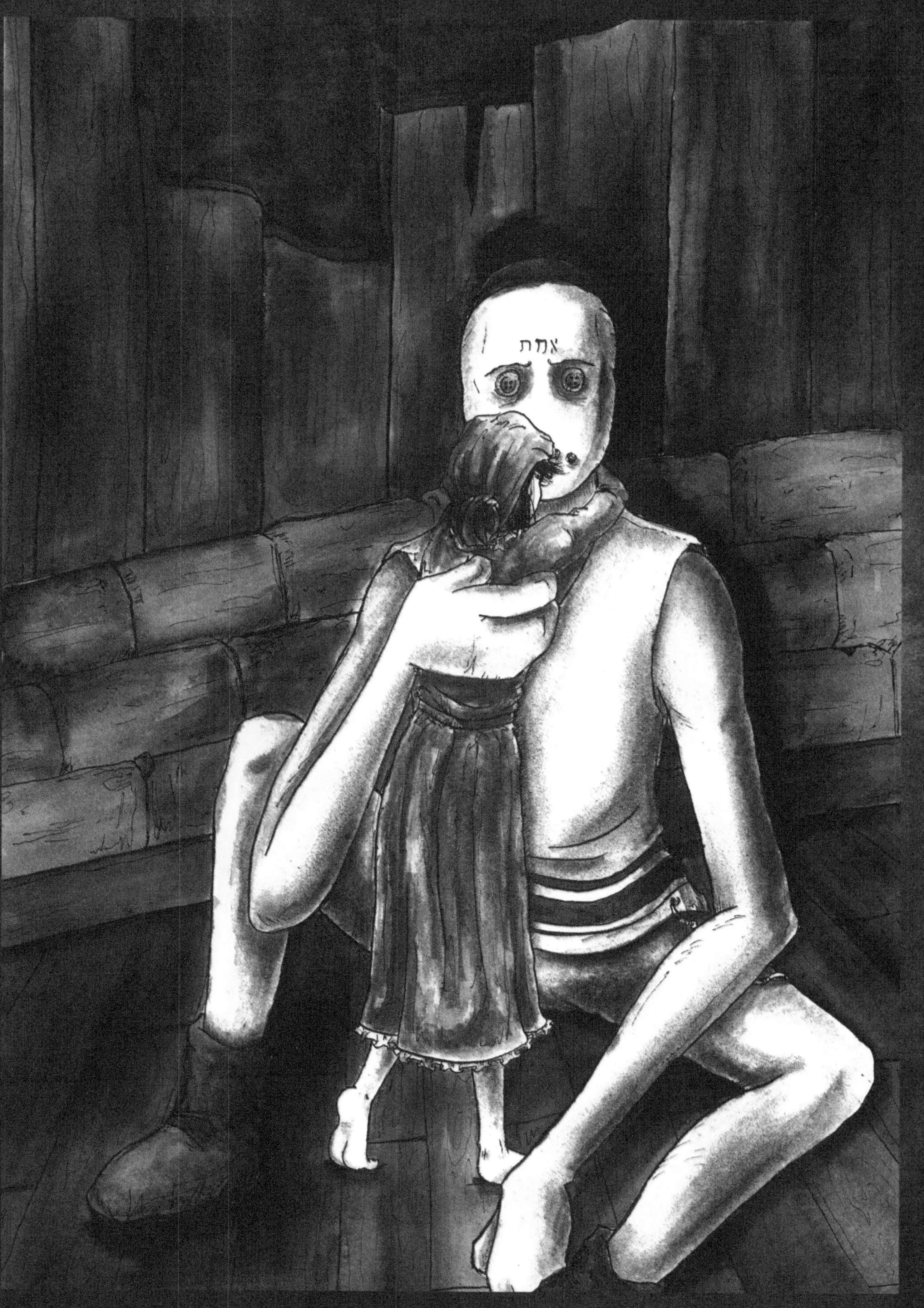
אמת

For a long time, the two of them let only their smiles speak. Shortly after, they returned to their places to continue their talk on a much lighter note. Eventually, Tzeitel fell into a deep sleep. Avi did what he could to make her comfortable and then left the old broken home to do something that he had not done for a long time. He went out into the forgotten village and began tidying up. All the while he came to the decision that Tzeitel, who had become the most beautiful thing in the world to him, was his chance for a new purpose. He would never leave her and always keep her safe. Avi found an old broom and began to sweep the cavern floor. And as he did, he sung the Shema, but only once. After he was finished, he stopped and thought about something else.

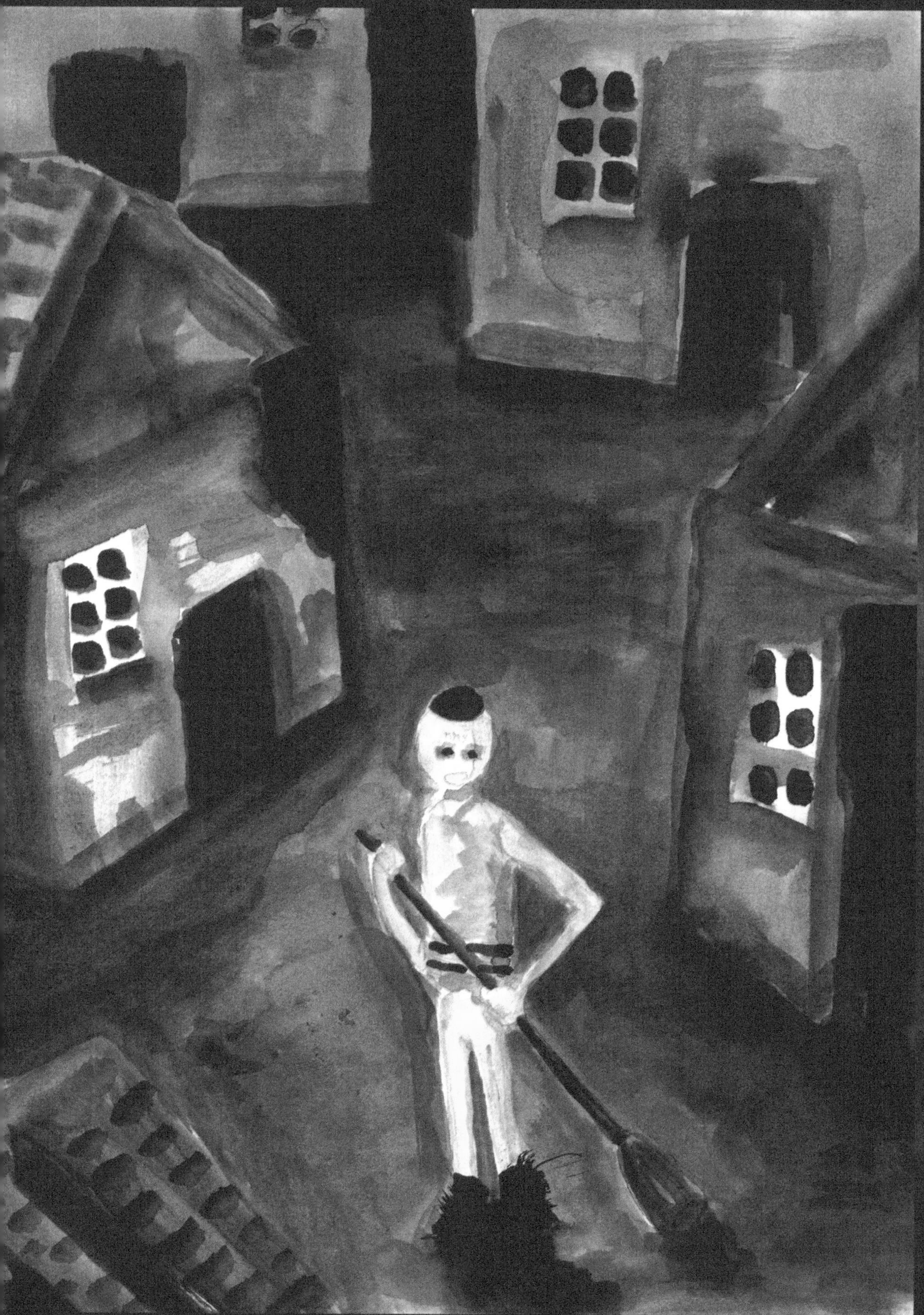

Chapter Four

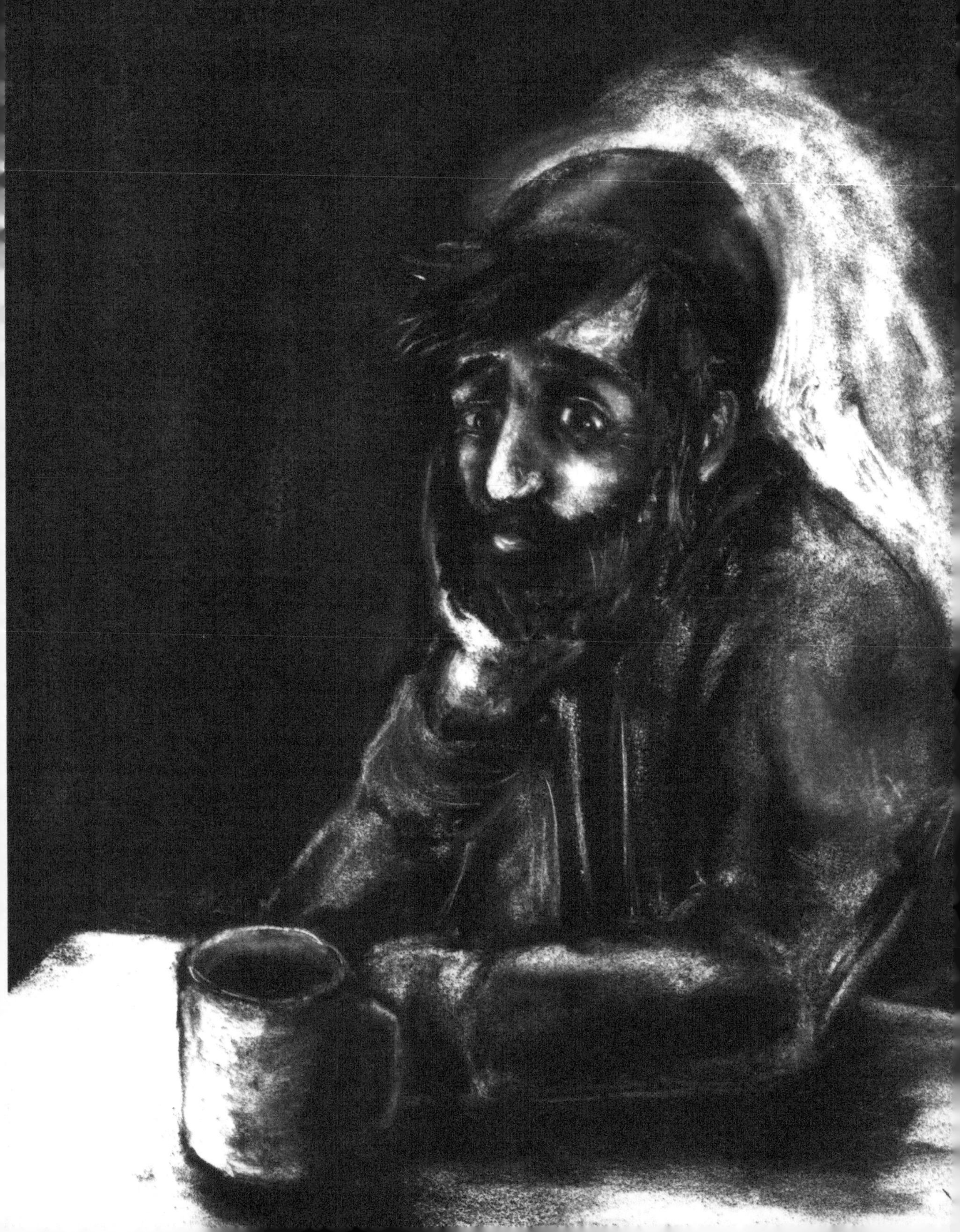

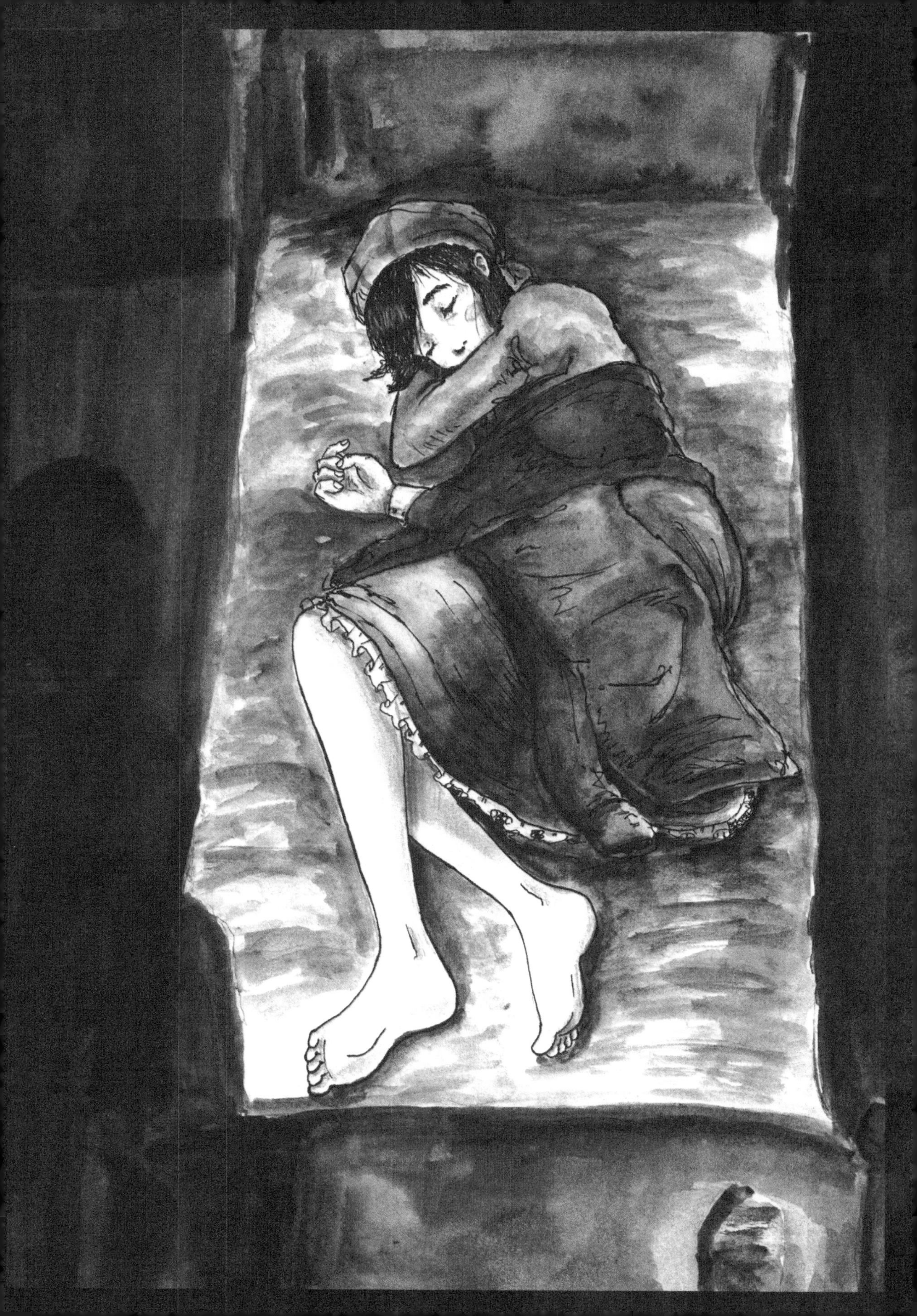

Tzeitel awoke sometime the following day, as I mentioned earlier. It was past midday when she did, as her father had not been there to make sure that she had risen at a decent hour. That was the topic of Tzeitel's first waking thought: her father. Lying flat on the musty bed, she gazed straight up at the partial ceiling and the top of the cavern canopy. This sight is what made her realize that she was not dreaming, and that her poor father was probably a nervous wreck by now. After recalling her father, she recalled the conversation she had with Avi the night before. This made her not want to get up and the sight of the house she was in made that desire even worse. She wondered how she could face the day knowing all her father had sacrificed to keep her safe. What she couldn't understand was that it was all because she was a Jew. She was just about to give into despair when she turned on her side, curled up, and hugged her legs. But in so doing she noticed that she was partially buried in her now dry winter clothes. She bolted into a sitting position and thought about what time it was. She knew that Avi probably had been awake for hours.

Tzeitel got out of bed and stretched out the kinks of sleep. Her legs were not used to walking, having been in a bed for so long, that she decided to sit down while getting dressed. It was much warmer than it had been the day before (or days before), so she didn't bother with all of her layers. After she got dressed an awful noise emitted from her stomach, so she decided that the best course of action would be to find something to eat. Whatever form that would take she did not know, but was open to suggestion.

The first thing she noticed when she exited the house, was that the entire cave looked a lot cleaner, if such a thing was possible. Rubble was stacked neatly in the unused homes, pebbles, glass, the myriad assortment of other miscellaneous refuse had been swept away, and it appeared as if someone had attempt to dust the buildings. With its new clean appearance, and bits of warm natural light pouring in through places here and there, the place almost looked majestic. Tzeitel would have believed that, if it were not for the reason why the place had been ruined and forgotten in the first place.

Tzeitel began walking aimlessly in an attempt to locate Avi. She knew that the best course of action would be to further assess her current situation, then to formulate a plan to return home to her father. But as she continued to roam the cave, much as she had previously done, she became less and less concerned with this idea. Without the Shema to follow, and a more peaceful look to the place, Tzeitel's childish curiosity had been captured. Similar to what she did with Avi, she began to imagine the names of people who had lived in the houses. She made up families and their jobs. She imagined walking past the tailor's shop, saying hello to an arbitrary passersby, and getting affectionate looks from the schoolboys as they went on their ways. It made her happy because it reminded her of her own home now lost. But all of her day dreams and fantasies soon consumed her as she walked through the many chambers, vaults, passages and halls. She soon came to an area of the cave untouched by anyone since the elements had buried it in the earth.

It was very quiet there.

She came to an abrupt stop as her day dreaming ceased, in favor of reality. The place made her feel uncomfortable, try as she might to ignore it. She remembered why she was walking in the first place and hoped that she would find Avi soon.

The first thing that she noticed in this new place was how different the buildings were. Although these were also in ruins, they had not become so in the same way as the others. The windows of these buildings had not been smashed. They had no smoke or fire damage, and they were not nearly as messy. She soon resumed her walk, only slower this time. She noticed that none of the door frames had mezuzahs and there were no Stars of David here or there. Jews had not lived there. Tzeitel's advance ended at this thought, and what happened next, she will never be able to explain.

Nothing in the place had changed, but suddenly a rush of intense fear came over her. She felt frozen in place and it seemed as though the entire vastness of the chamber and all it contained began to contort. Like a trick mirror, she saw the forms around her distort ever so slightly. And then she felt like she was being watched. At first she felt it was only one person, but soon more followed. After a brief moment she felt as though a hundred people with a hundred terrible faces were advancing towards her, trying to suffocate her.

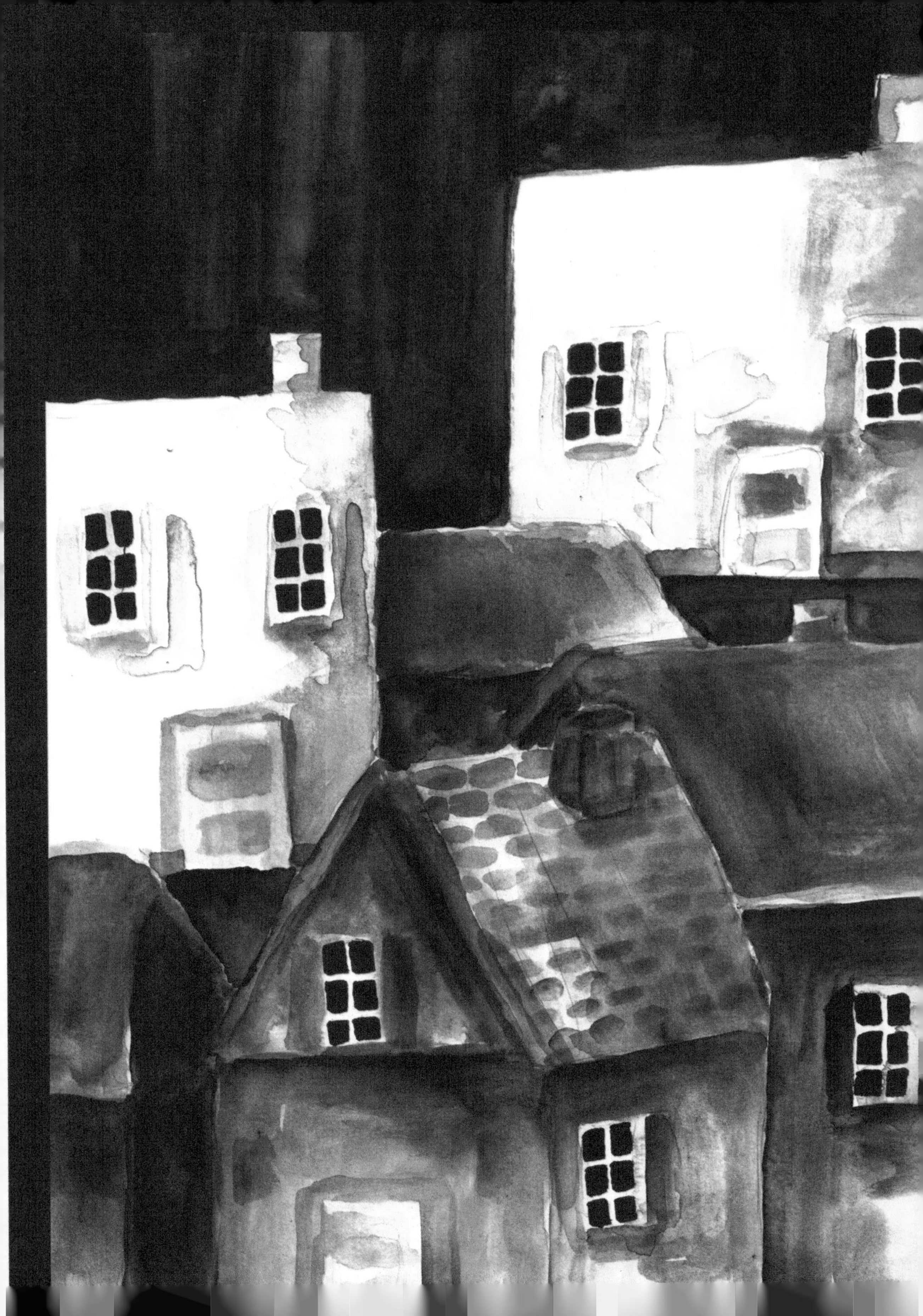

She did not know why these imaginary people were so terrifying, but she broke into a run, and then a sprint. Her bare feet smacked against the stones and dirt of the cavern floor, stinging them as she went. She ran because she had suddenly remembered a time when she was a very small child and had wandered out of the Jewish quarter of her old village. The looks that the imaginary cave-people were giving her were the same looks the goyim from her old village had given her. They were in no way friendly. It had troubled her then—that people could look that way upon a child.

She continued to run. Faint whispers from talks between her father and visitors to their cottage came into her mind. Although she never actually heard them, she saw the way her father looked after they were over. Now that she was older, she knew what they were about. For as hard as we try, and even though they may not understand at the time, nothing can be kept from a child. Living away from it all did not stop Tzeitel from picking up on the subtle suggestions of trouble that her father exhibited. She felt as if she knew what would happen to her, should these imaginary people catch her.

As she ran, she soon spotted a passage to her left and darted towards it as fast as she could. In so doing she lost her footing and tripped, falling forward and giving her knees a good skinning on the hard and jagged stones which littered the cavern floor. She let out a cry and as she attempted to scramble to her feet, a great force caught her up, and flew her away from the place she was in. Her eyes were shut as tightly as she could muster, and she clung to whatever had taken her. She knew that it would not hurt her, and as soon as she was taken through the passage, she could feel her fear slip. This new place was warm and inviting. The feeling of persecution and rage was gone. She slowly opened her eyes to find that it was Avi who had again rescued her, and as she regained her composure, she felt embarrassed for reacting in such a way to her own imagination. Her arms were wrapped around the golem's massive neck, and she buried her face in it, attempting to hide her tears.

"I'm sorry," he said to her softly, "I should have told you about that place. I did not think you would go there."

Tzeitel said nothing to her friend. She only continued to soak in the moment. It reminded her of the way her father had held her in his arms after the time he had found her outside the Jewish quarter of their old village.

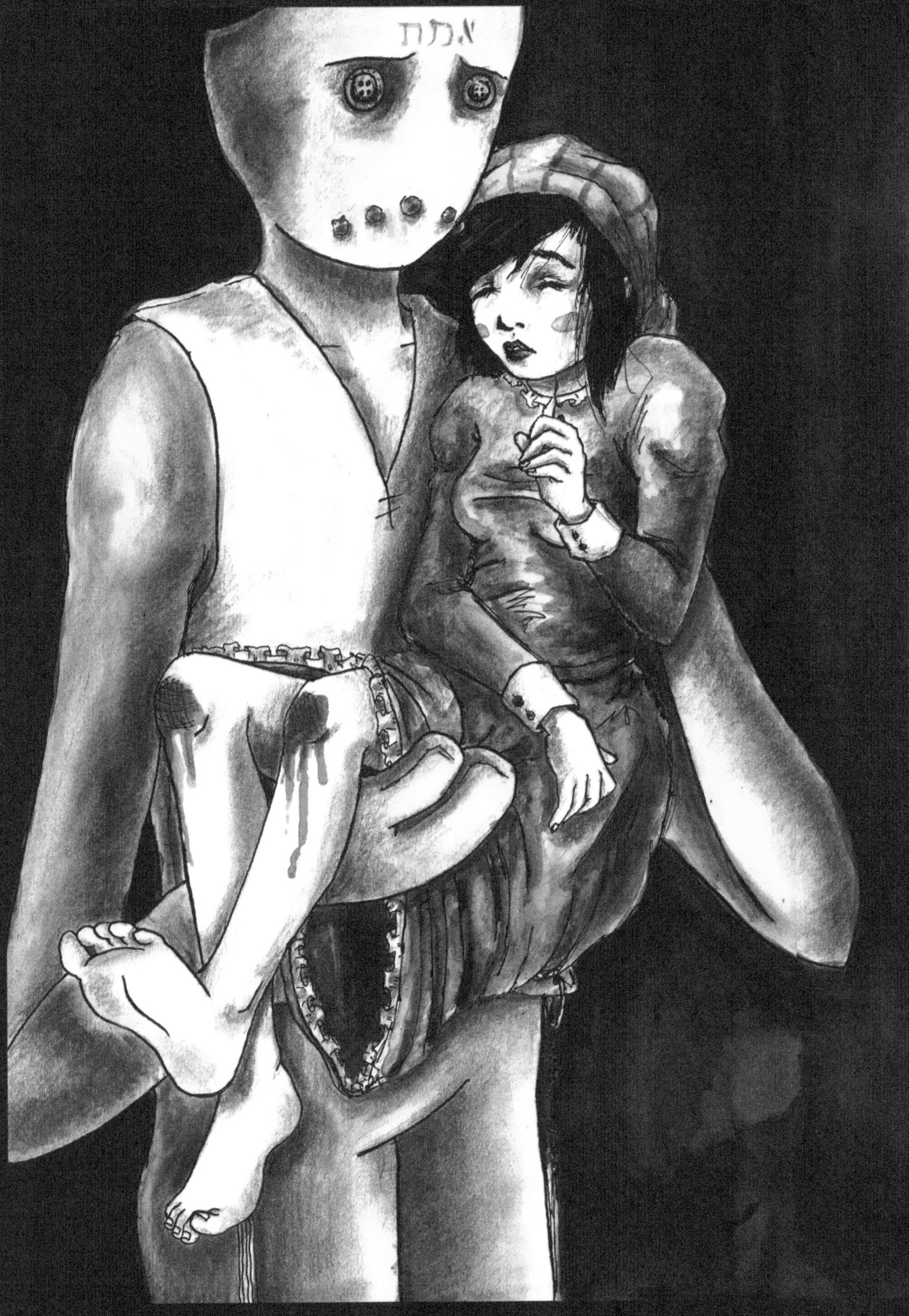
אמת

As the creature continued to cradle the tiny girl in his arms, he noticed the injuries that she had sustained. He saw her blood and he listened to her breath and thought he remembered something about his past. But just as quickly as it came, it left him. He held Tzeitel a little tighter, hoping that it would return. He carried her into another chamber, but nothing came into his mind.

It was not long before he stopped walking. Tzeitel did not see where it was that he was taking her, as she remained in his arms; her face buried the entire time. When she noticed that he had stopped, she turned her head to take a look. This new chamber was large and empty save for a small pool of water in the middle. Light crept in through a vast number of openings along the chamber. She was placed at the water's edge, and without so much as a thought, she instantly submerged her feet. The water was strangely warm, and she wiggled her toes and gently kicked it about. She pulled up her dress and looked at the cuts on her bare knees.

"What was that place, Avi?" she asked after a short but deep silence.

"It is a place that I never go," he answered. "It is the only part of this cave that harbors angry and lost spirits."

"I wonder why?" Tzeitel mused. "I would think that would be the only part of the cave that was pure. Why is it that the Jews who lived here do not haunt this place?"

"Perhaps it is because of the hate the people who lived there felt. Hate is a hard thing to let go of. It takes so much work to harbor."

Tzeitel considered the angry ghosts as she drew scoops of water from the pool and washed the blood from her knees.

The two companions fell silent again, not knowing what to say. It was undeniable to Tzeitel that Avi had something to do with what had happened to the village in the cave, and it was undeniable to her that what had happened was a pogrom. It was then that she decided her father could wait. Avi needed her help to discover his past and find out what had really happened to the place that they were in. It was not right to her that such a kind being was not at peace with itself.

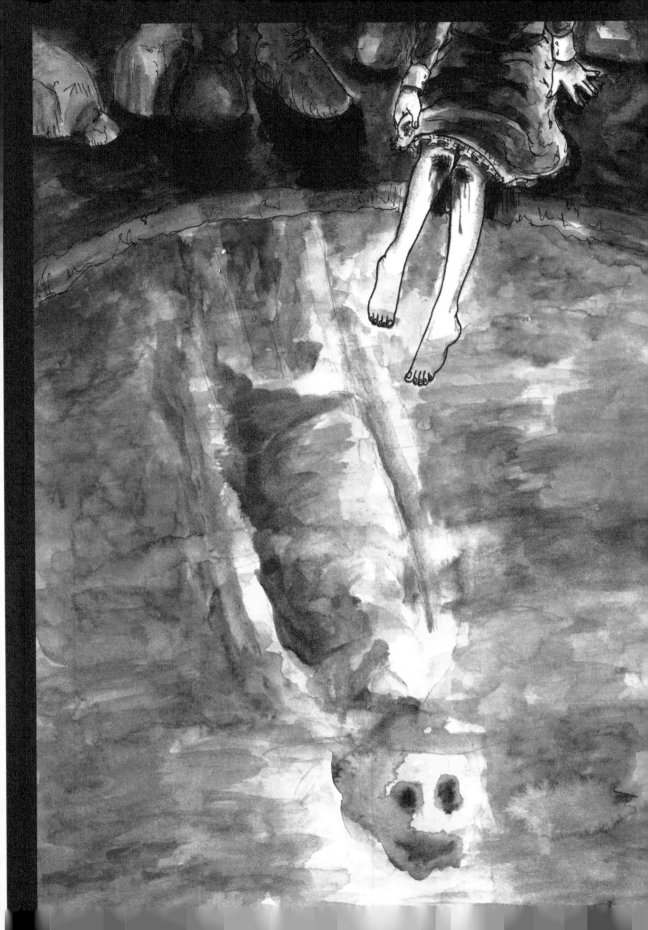

As she thought about this, she became distracted by the soothing feeling of the water running over her burning knees and down her legs. She slowly kicked her feet and watched as her tiny toes submerged and reemerged. She could not remember the last time that she had a proper bath, and decided that must be seen to. She kindly asked Avi to wait outside the chamber for her, which he did. The golem lumbered away through a different passage and left his companion to undress.

Tzeitel stood up and carefully undressed down to her nightgown, which had belonged to her mother. She wore it underneath her dress for an extra layer of warmth, and decided to bathe with it on should any ghosts come after her. She tossed her other clothes aside and slowly entered the pool, enjoying every second as it came.

The pool was much deeper than it looked, and soon she found that the water level had risen to her waist. Not wanting to be caught by a sudden drop, she carefully probed the bottom with her toes as slowly waded about. Once she was satisfied that her bath consisted of no more inherent risks, she allowed herself to relax and quickly submerged into the water. She remained under for as long as she could hold her breath, and then shot back up. She began to wash and her thoughts wandered over long distances, visiting many topics and ideas.

She could not remember what she was thinking about at the time when she realized that she was sinking deeper into the water, but once she did, it was too late. She did not even have time to scream before she was completely pulled under and off to places unknown.

Avi was not sure how long it had been when he became concerned and decided to risk checking up on her. He did not know what length of time was customary for a young woman to bathe, but he was sure it had been far too long. He slowly waddled into the chamber covering his eyes with his massive hands and calling Tzeitel's name.

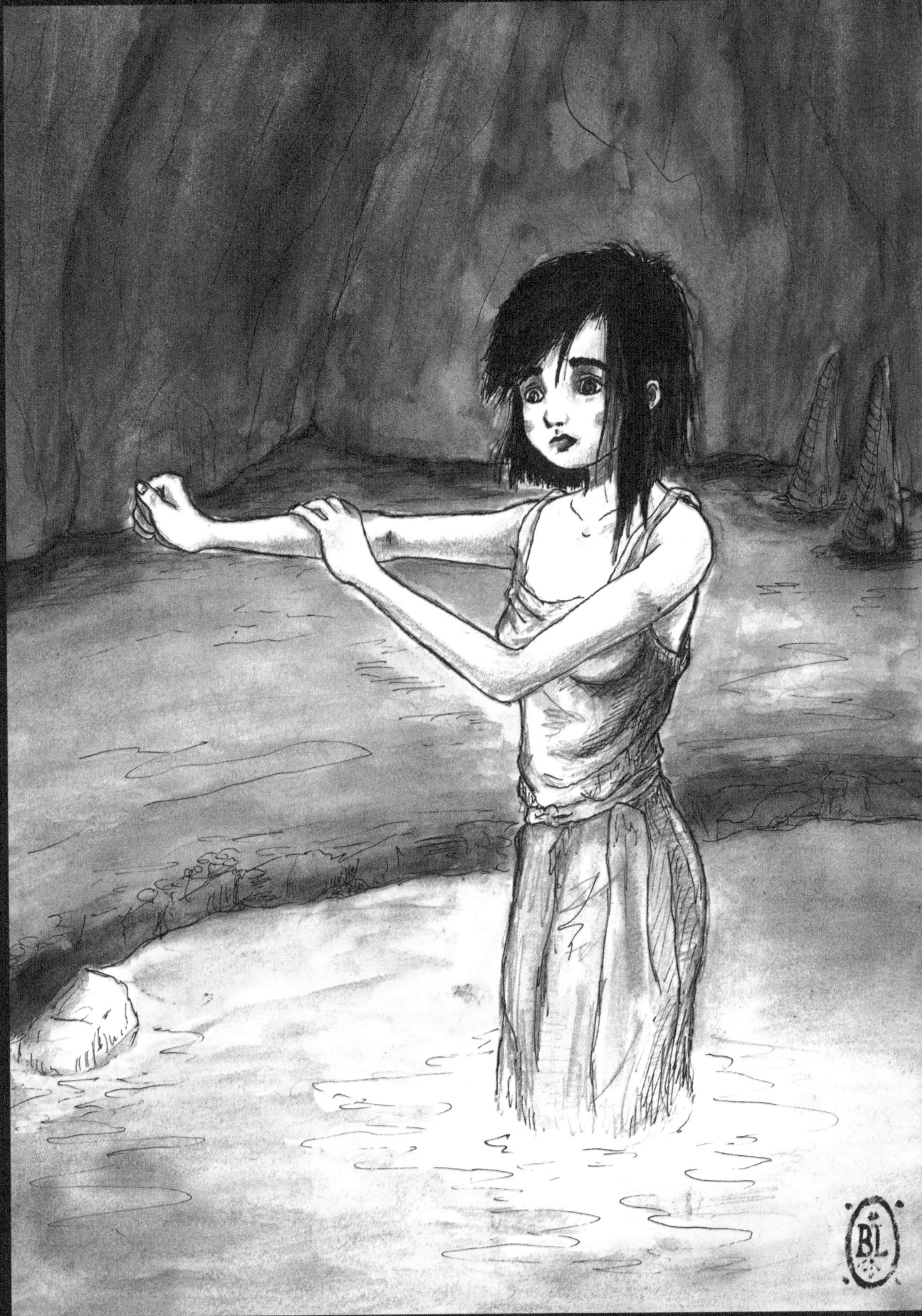

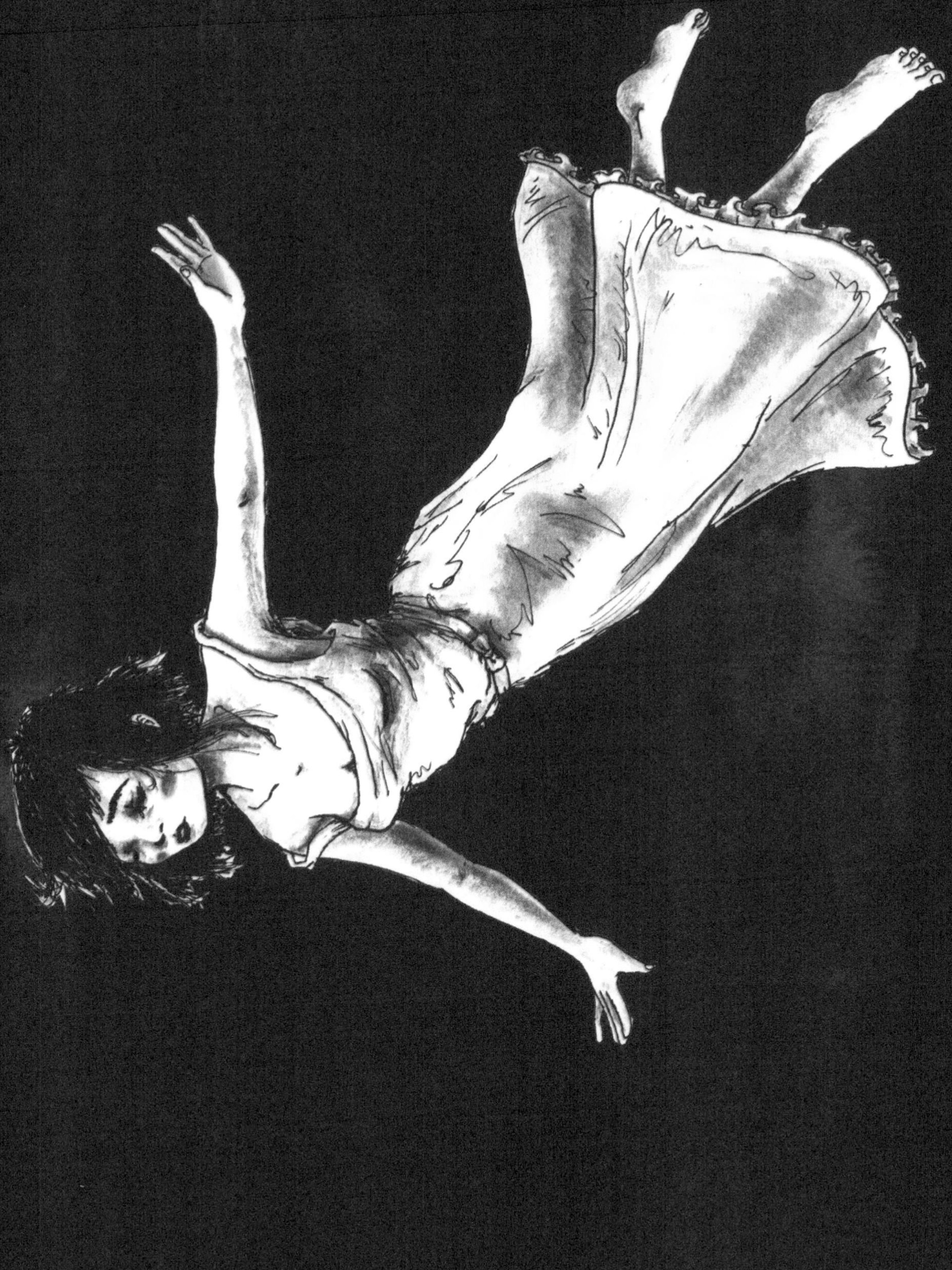

Chapter Five

At first all fear she felt as she had sunk under was gone. She spent some unknown time simply drifting in an indescribable place, watch the indescribable shapes and masses pass her by. But then, all at once, this sudden tranquility vanished and she began to scream and weep, but no sound came from her. She grew terribly cold and then all went black. And then she saw her father.

In an instant she was standing in the doorway of her old home in her old village, bundled up in clothes to the point where you could barely tell that there was a little girl underneath all of them. Standing some distance away, a typical distance a parent stands when they deliver difficult news to their children, was her father. She could not remember if she was leaving or just arriving, but regardless, she soon found herself outside retracing long gone steps. It was the day her father sent her out to purchase supplies for their move, but he had not told her that. When she came back, their dearest possessions were packed away into a motley assortment of containers: boxes, dilapidated suitcases, jars, and so forth. They ate supper without speaking, and late in the night her father woke her. He had her hastily dress and led her outside to a cart. It was full with their things and Tzeitel was coaxed onto it. She tried as hard as she could to go back to sleep, put the bumps of the road kept her awake as her father drew the cart himself. Looking back on it, she had known that day would come.

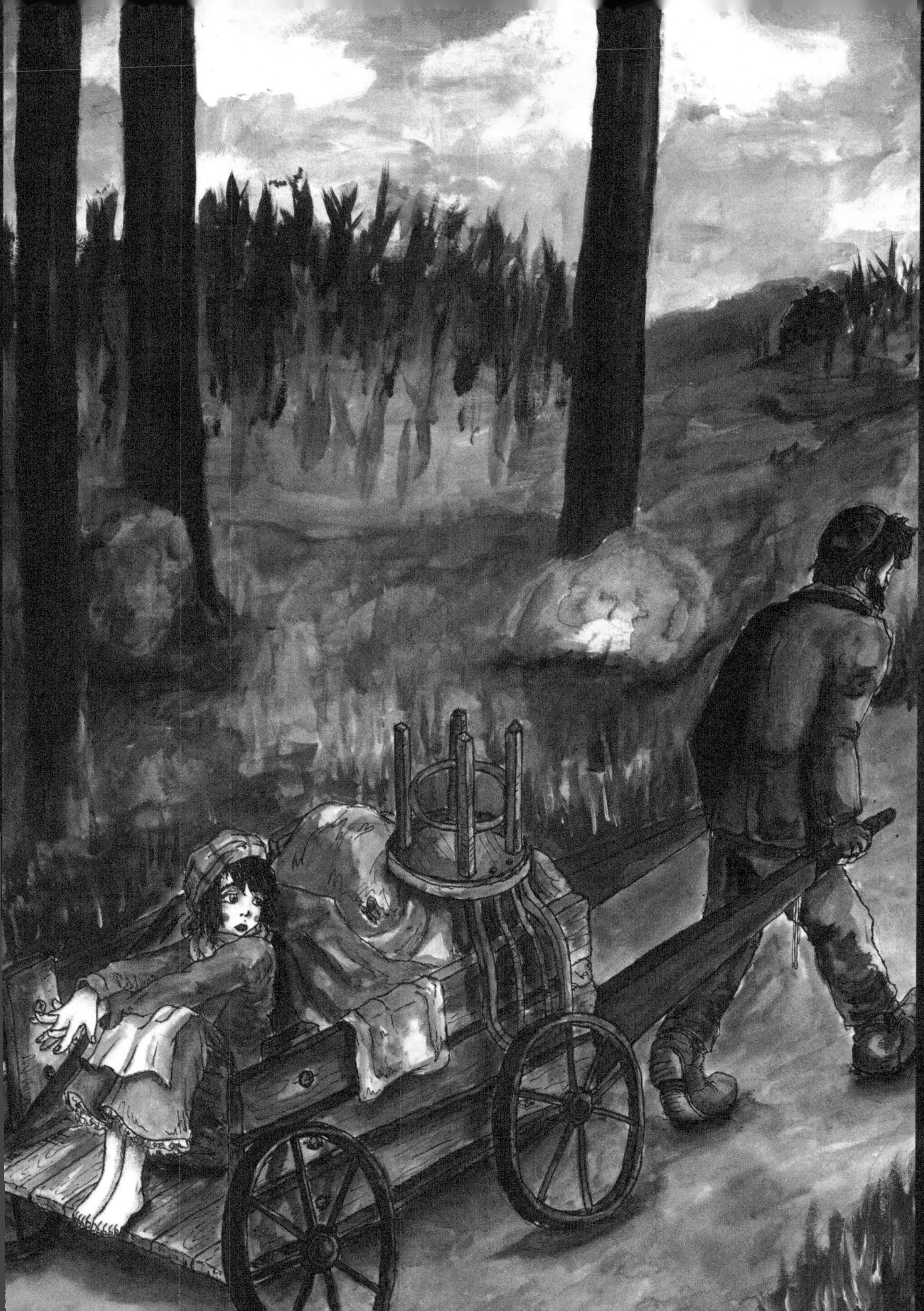

As Tzeitel resurfaced, the first thing she saw was gold. It was all around her and it dripped down her shivering arms. She saw her hands submerged in it and then titled her head towards her chest. Her eyes followed it down past her abdomen, across her thighs, and finally to her knees. She darted her gaze about and discovered that she was in a pond complete with lily pads, weeds, and other plant life. Her eyes widened in fright when she realized that she had been under water and could not remember the last time she took a breath. With this she scrambled across the few meters between her and the pond's edge, collapsed on the grass, gasped, and coughed furiously. She took in a deep and fretful breath, and then another and another. Her eyes had been closed most of the time, but when she rolled over and opened them, she saw a sky that was not filled with grey clouds and dimly lit. She saw a sky filled with the wildly beautiful colors of a summer sunrise. The reflection had made the water appear gold. And it was not snow or rock that she lay upon, it was soft wild grass. The joy of another long, hard winter ending filled her with bliss. She got up and buried her tender feet into the lush green about her. She wiggled her toes trying to soak up every bit of the sensation. She wondered for a long time after that if she had died and this was paradise. But the feeling did not last long. Her heart sank as she remembered Avi and worried about where he was. This made her decide that she wasn't really dead. If she really had died and gone to paradise, then the thought of being away from Avi would probably have not troubled her at all. With that she rose to her feet and decided that something had to be done. What that was, however, she did not know.

Even though she did not want to leave this place for the sake that it was summer here and winter back in the cave, she eventually decided that, perhaps, it was best to be lost in place she could give reason to concerning its existence. She entered the pool with the intent of returning, but found it only to be ankle deep. She wiggled her toes in the water in a mild form of disappointment and confusion. She then decided that if she waited long enough, Avi might put two and two together and come after her. She sat down next to the pond and waited for a few hours, occupying herself with the joy of summer and the refreshing breezes as they came. But it soon became apparent to her that she had no food and no shelter, and a lack of all those things in the wild spelled danger. Finally she made up her mind that the best thing to do was move on and find out where she was. So she started walking and soon found a road nearby. It was obvious that her best bet would be to follow it so she did.

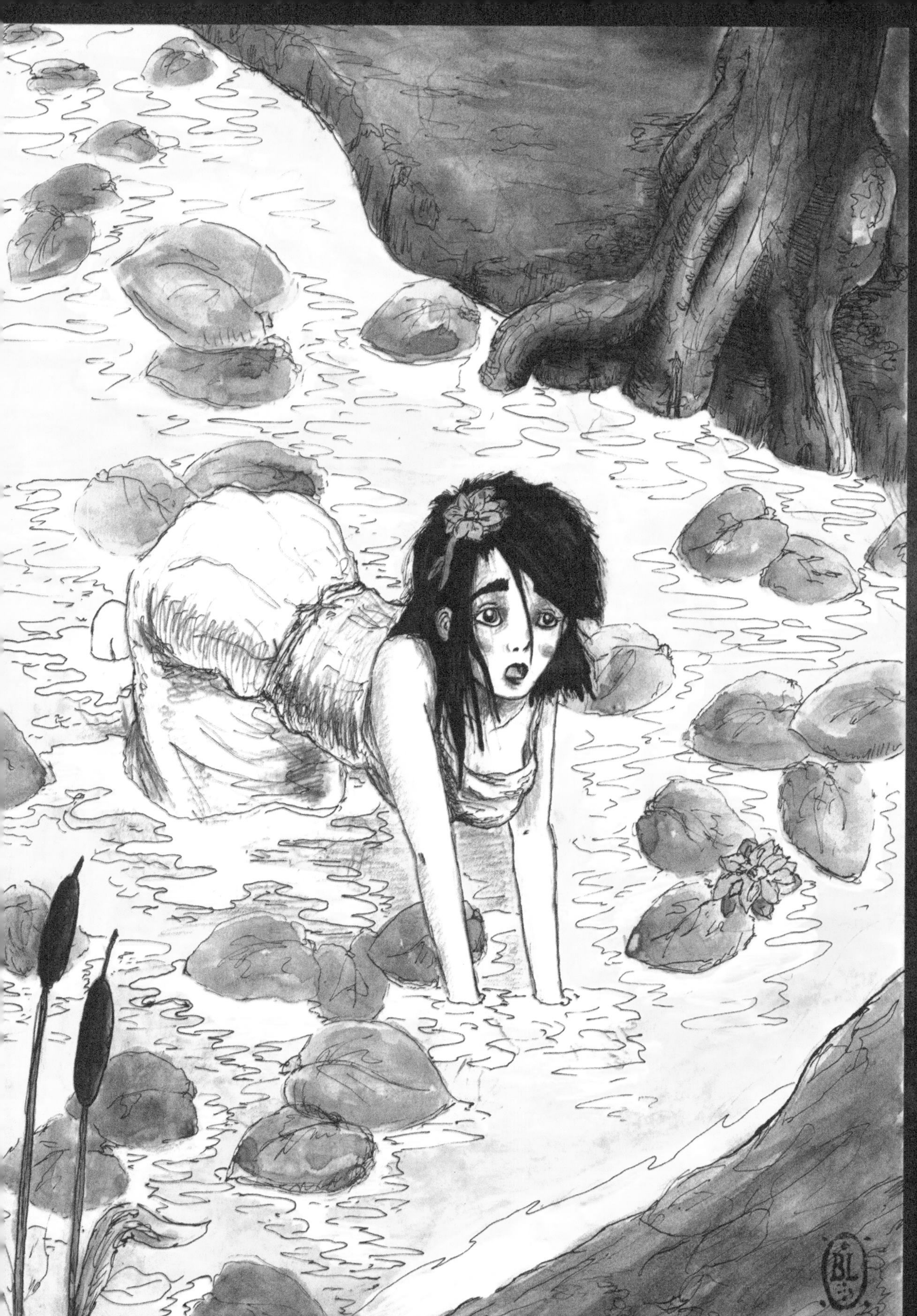

After some time, Tzeitel spotted two men with fishing rods heading towards her in the distance. A rush of excitement came over her at finding someone here, as she was beginning to feel as though she would never get anywhere. She found herself breaking into a run and then a sprint. Of course, she did not at that point consider the sight she presented to them. She only realized it when she reached them, and after the men remembered how to talk. It was not every day that you'd see a girl Tzeitel's age barreling down a road, wearing nothing but a night gown, and screaming the word "hello" as if she had not seen another person in years. After taking that into consideration, you could say that the men acted appropriately when they saw her. They said nothing as Tzeitel reached them, bent over, braced her knees, and in between heavy pants for air managed to sputter out a nearly incoherent, "Shalom." It was only out of that certain kind of oblivious politeness that they returned her greeting. Beyond that nothing was said for a long time. It was about this time that Tzeitel realized what a shock she had brought them with her presence. She addressed them while their mouths still hung slightly ajar.

"Excuse me," she said as she lifted the top of her night gown a little higher and tried to push her hair back. "I think that I need help."

The two men were obviously Jewish and they became less apprehensive when they realized that Tzeitel was too. This was only because of the terrible things that could have happened, should they have been seen with a non-Jew in the same state that our heroine was in. One of them gave her his jacket and then they walked on either side of her as they listened to her story. Tzeitel did not notice that they were walking, nor did she notice the village she was being led to. She could only focus on her story that sounded absolutely ridiculous to her new companions. As the men listened, they both independently decided that she really did need help because she was delusional. The three of them made their way into the village and again, the men independently decided that the best thing to do was bring this strange young girl to see the Rabbi.

When they told her this, Tzeitel was pleased, as she suddenly remembered the Rabbi of her old village. She felt happy knowing that she would speak to a man who would possibly be friendly, receptive, and had knowledge of strange happenings. Surely, if anyone could help her, it would be a Rabbi.

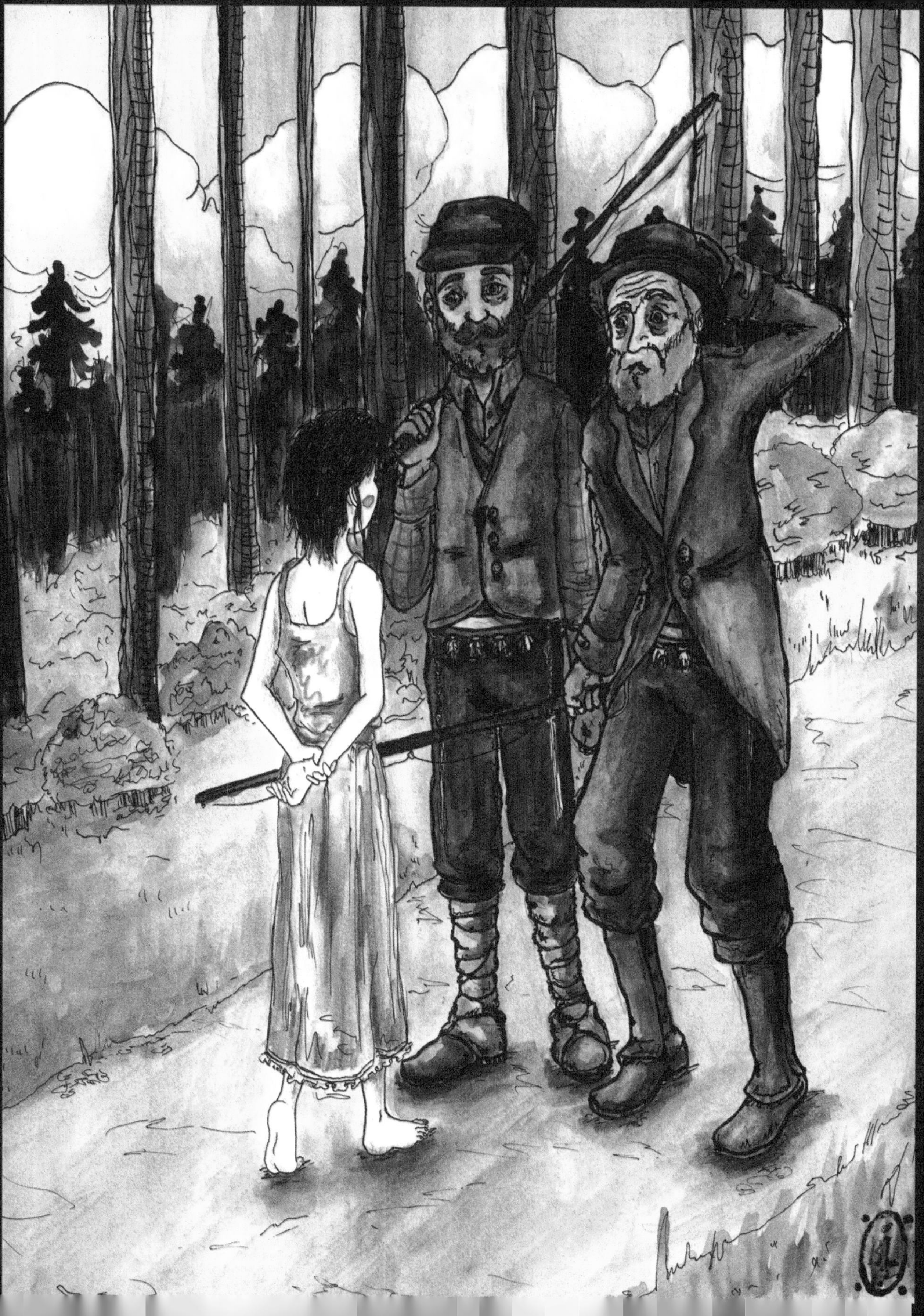

The two men led her to a small and modest synagogue. They all went inside and one of the men asked for the Rabbi. Tzeitel's situation had to be explained several times and to several different people before she found herself waiting in the Rabbi's study. Tzeitel waited impatiently and fussed with a tichel that someone had given to her along the way. Apparently the village's Rabbi had been acting strange lately. He had recently taken to disappearing for long amounts of time in his study, but when someone went to see him, they found that he was not there. Of course no one told Tzeitel that no one knew where the Rabbi was. In truth, everyone had been a little disturbed by her presence and felt that it was just best if the Rabbi dealt with it whenever, wherever, and however that would occur. As far as anyone was concerned, Tzeitel was speaking with him at that very moment.

Being the kind of girl that she was, Tzeitel was not one to stew in quiet indignation. The time she spent fidgeting with the hems of her new jacket and curling her toes in agitation was short lived. Snooping through the various different books and esoteric objects which inhabited the Rabbi's study became her new outlet to express irritation. In the innocent way that only girls her age can get away with, she began pulling books off of shelves and paging through them. She collected little bits of interesting information before returning them to their homes, but in the wrong order. She would pick up little trinkets and absentmindedly set them down wherever she pleased as the next object grabbed her attention. All in all, it greatly calmed her down, which helped her react in a much more reasonable way when she came across a curious weathered book on the Rabbi's desk.

She picked up the old tome and opened it to discover that it was all hand written——presumably by the Rabbi, which was her guess. It contained a multitude of strange scribbles and notes as well as diagrams and drawings. She became engrossed in it after recognizing a few of the drawings. Tzeitel had become so focused on the baffling coincidences the book contained that she did not notice when the Rabbi entered the room through a hidden passage. He approached her in a controlled fury and demanded to know what she was doing. Normally Tzeitel would have been taken by complete surprise at an event such as this and would have jumped into the air after giving a little shriek. But during this specific surprise she experienced in her life, she only turned around as calm as ever. She held the book to the Rabbi, revealing a drawing that was on the page.

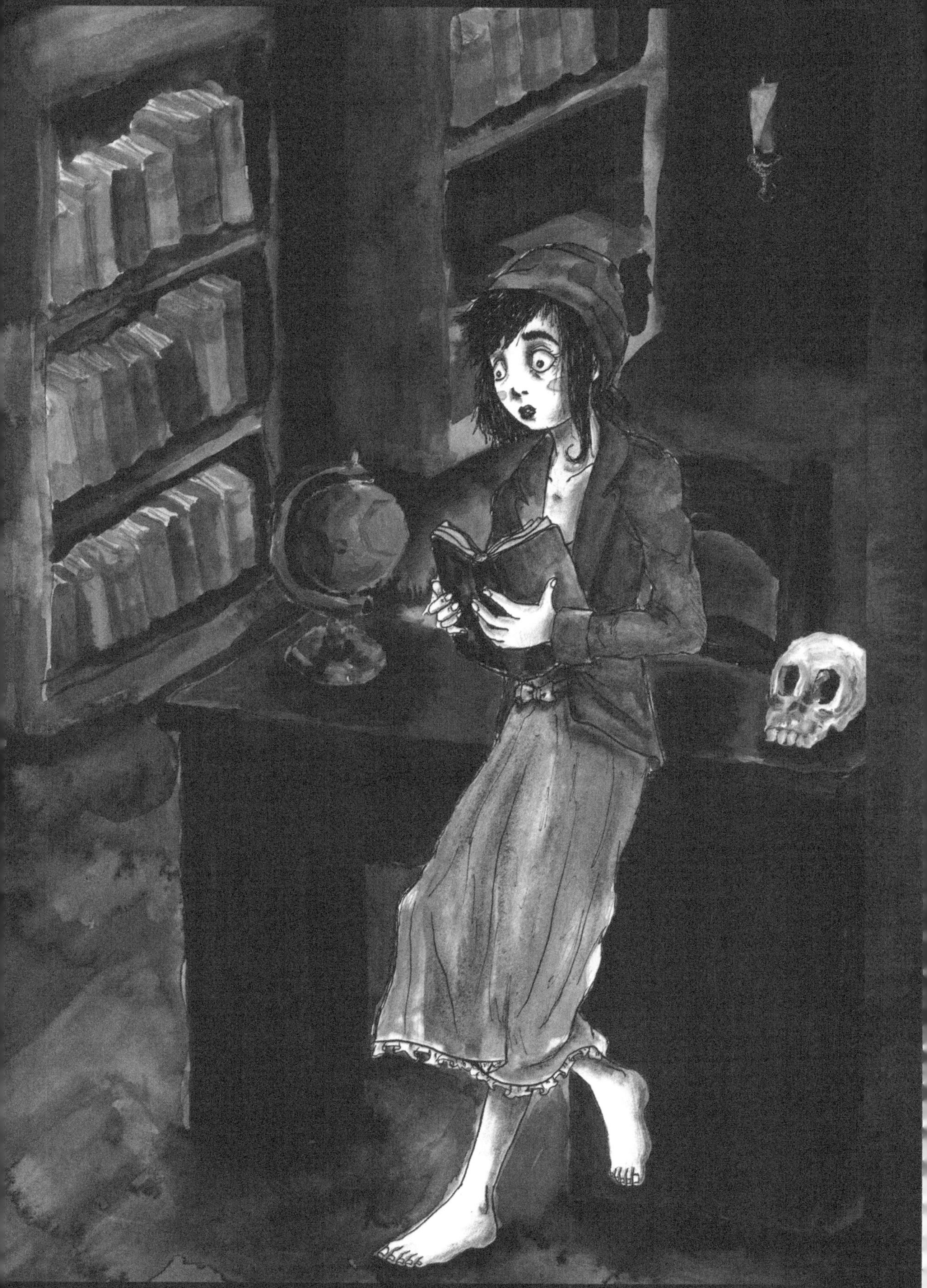

"Why is there a picture of Avi in here?" she asked firmly with a completely straight face.

The Rabbi's face fell after turning white. His right hand groped around the air behind him, and when it found the back of his chair, he pulled himself onto it with a clumsy slump. He took off his spectacles and tugged at his long and wrinkled face. Then he realized that he had no idea what to say.

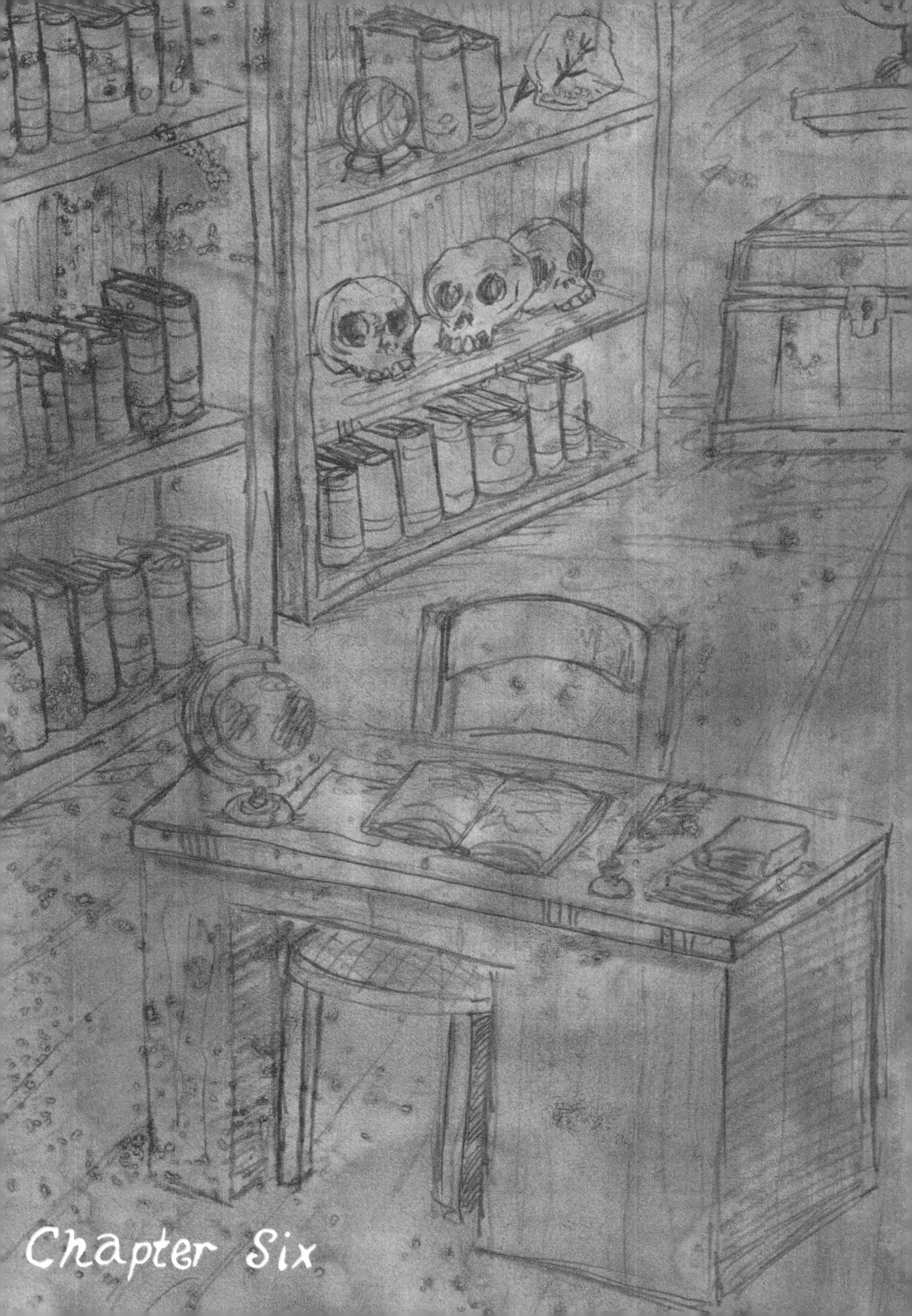

Chapter Six

Tzeitel's face was frozen in a stern and mildly angry determination. The Rabbi suddenly felt any authority he could have had in the situation slip away into nothing. He looked into the strange girl's eyes which still bore traces of delicacy. He still had no idea what to say. Even though he had no idea why she called the drawing "Avi," it was obvious to him that she knew what it was. This deeply troubled him and he had to fight against the urge to get up and run away as far as he could.

He could see that the girl was growing more and more impatient with his silence. Her out stretched arm began to shake and he feared that she might drop the book and damage it.

"Well?" Tzeitel demanded again. "Are you going to answer my question or not?"

She did not mean to be rude and the Rabbi knew this. And even though, for just a moment, he wondered if she was an angel, he decided that his work could not be compromised.

"I think that I should ask," he began in a low toned, calm voice as he stood up trying to regain an authoritative stance, "how it is that you know what that drawing is of."

"It's my friend, Avi," Tzeitel said, refusing to hand the book over as the Rabbi reached for it. She pulled her arm back and clenched the old tome to her chest.

"This friend of yours, um, Avi," the Rabbi said slowly, "Do you know what he is?"

"A golem," was the girl's stern answer.

"How do you know what that is?"

"Avi told me."

It went without saying that this was indeed the most bizarre day that the Rabbi had had in recent memory. One moment he was off attending to his business, and the next thing he knew there was a peculiar girl in his study paging through his most private of thoughts. He had never seen her before and she was there without any explanation. Most of all, she knew certain things that he was sure no one did.

"Perhaps," the Rabbi ventured, "it would be best if you just told me who you are and how you got here."

"My name is Tzeitel," was how she began her tale.

After everything had been said, the Rabbi did not know what to think. Was G-d trying to tell him something? Did this girl mark the arrival of the Messiah? All things considered, the Rabbi eventually thought, anything is possible. Had it not been for the fact that Tzeitel knew what the golem was, the Rabbi would have taken her for a loon, given her something to eat and shooed her away. Had the Rabbi not been creating such a creature himself, he would not have believed her. His question now was how to proceed.

The Rabbi found it strange that Tzeitel had reacted in the way she did to his most specific drawing of the golem. One might say that she really did know this creature, but how then did she meet him? The Rabbi was perplexed because he had just recently completed this creature and had not yet activated it. It had been living in his secret chamber along with all his other tucked away experiments. His creature had not been seen by anyone, nor did anyone know that he had made it. Suspicion ran rampant throughout the synagogue about his long hours spent in an unknown place. It seemed possible that perhaps it had spilled out into the community causing the birth of rumors. It seemed possible that perhaps one of the children decided to make a wild guess and confront him about it. This seemed the most logical of possibilities, except that the Rabbi knew all of the Jewish children in the village. He had never seen Tzeitel before and visitors were already known about days before their arrival. Tzeitel also did not speak like someone trying to make a mockery of you. Her eyes were the most serious he had ever seen. And to call it Avi and make up a completely impossible story to explain it? The Rabbi decided that, in all probability, she must be telling the truth. This terrified him more than anything he had ever experienced. Something had to be done.

The Rabbi glanced over towards her and noticed that her stance had faltered. He had been lost in thought and did not know for how long. Catching her in a less aggressive pose prompted him to remember that his work must not be compromised. He puffed out his chest, furrowed his brow and shot forward his long and weather hand.

"May I please have my book back now?" is what he said.

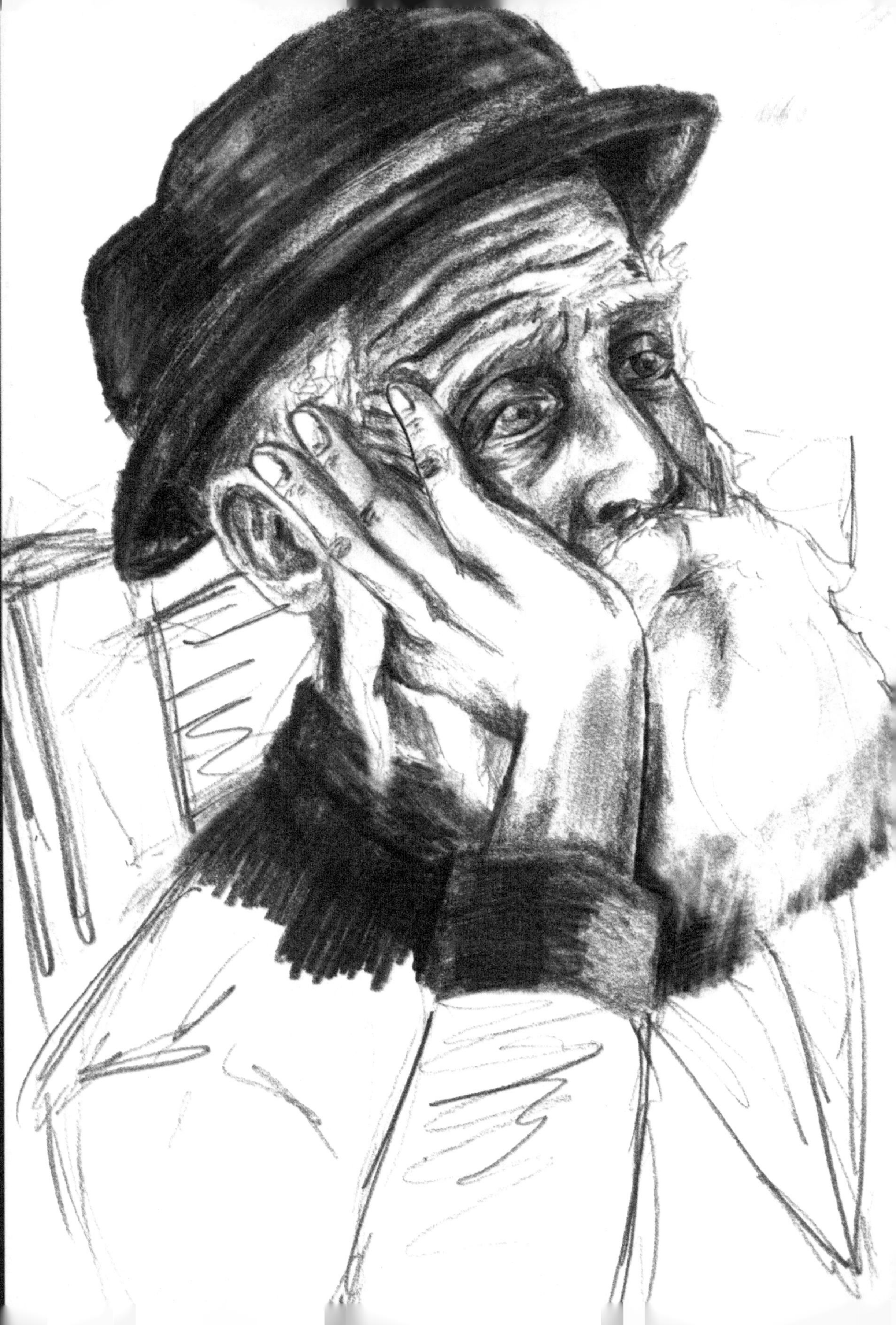

The Rabbi sent Tzeitel away after telling her that it was necessary to think on her tale. He told her to check back in a few hours. Tzeitel spent a good deal of that time sulking on the stoop of the synagogue before she decided to have a look around. She sat slouched over with her chin in her hands and her toes curled around the edge of the step. It was utterly obvious that the Rabbi knew something about Avi and Tzeitel was absolutely determined to find out what that was. But eventually, as does happen with all children in such situations, she grew bored with waiting and became distracted by the life of the village.

The people were nice enough, but word of her arrival and tale had already swept through the town: the strange young girl with a wild story. Many people thought that she was just lost and just plain crazy. Others thought that she had survived some sort of accident and that it had tainted her mind. But most of them simply did not have time for her. Everyone was busy with their daily tasks; their minds occupied by thoughts of the near future. When Tzeitel was tired of being treated in such ways, she returned to the synagogue. There she asked to see the Rabbi again, and was told that they did not know where he was.

This time she was not sent to wait in his study. This time she was sent to a corner and there she spent several more hours. After those hours had concluded, she was told to come back the next day if it was that important, and she spent the night in a small alley behind the synagogue. She found small amounts of old food discarded there and ate for the first time since the Shabbat dinner with her father the night she left. She woke up the next day stiff, dirty, and smelling rather unpleasant. She returned to the synagogue and continued to wait. When she asked if the Rabbi had returned, she was given only vague answers that really told her nothing. She was sent away again and spent more time out in the village.

It was obvious that the Rabbi was purposely trying to put her off. She decided that getting angry about it would not do, and that persistence would be the best way to proceed. She was a child after all, and knew how to get her way. It then became fine that the Rabbi would not see her, she could wait. She started to walk a little more confidently when she considered how the people at the synagogue would react if she started to cry the next time she showed up. This made her quietly giggle to herself.

With her new strategy in mind, Tzeitel decided that the best thing to do would be to relax a little. She recalled all the made up people she imagined in the cave in the forest, and began putting those invented names to the faces she encountered. At times she found it funny to see how her imagined characters matched up with these real ones. This caused her to discover a certain respect for a few, and made her laugh all the harder at the family scandals. Her only regret was that the looks she received from passing schoolboys were not at all what you might call affectionate.

It made her feel a lot better because this strange new place began to take on a familiarity to her. This was uncanny because many times she would pass a building and stop to wonder why. Was it just her childish games and imagination that made the place suddenly familiar, or was it something else? This began to worry her as she went. Suddenly she would see a mezuzah on a doorpost and would know that she had seen it before. These little instances of déjà vu only increased as her time in the village went on. The last episode made her blood run cold.

It had grown dark out when she found herself coming to a dead stop. The buildings had grown sparse in placement as she had walked, but all of a sudden they were dense again. She looked about and realized where she was. She was walking in the forgotten village in the cave, only it had not yet been forgotten. The particular part of village, where she now stood, was none other than the place which had been inhabited by angry spirits back in the cave. It was no longer the Jewish district that she was in. She gazed around at the buildings for only a moment, but it was all the time she needed to match these buildings to the ones burned into her memory. Before she knew what was happening, her heart sank she had broken into a maddening run. She knew what was going to happen and could no longer wait for the Rabbi.

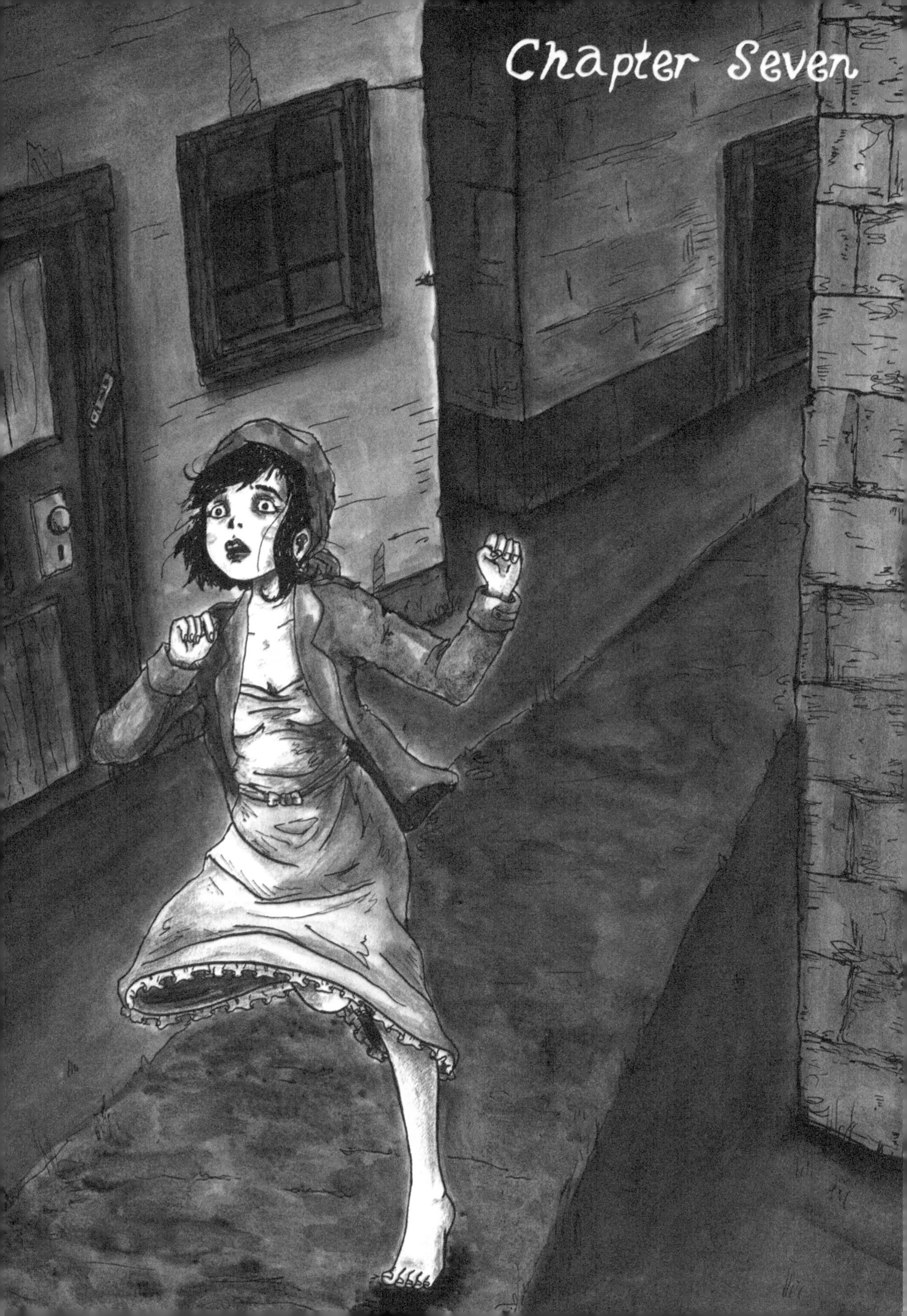
Chapter Seven

When she arrived back at the synagogue, she forced herself to calm down. Even though the fate of the Jewish district had become apparent to her, it would not do to simply barge in and demand to see the Rabbi at such an hour. Tzeitel took a deep breath and then sneaked around to the back of the synagogue and peered through a low window. After she was satisfied that no one was inside, she experienced further satisfaction when she discovered that the window she was spying through was not locked. She carefully lifted it up and, like a worm, slipped through. She miscalculated the distance to the floor and met it was a thud. After hastily scrambling to her feet, and ignoring her throbbing elbow, she scanned the area intently. She waited a few moments before making her way to the Rabbi's study. Of course, she thought, she could be wrong and would find that the Rabbi really was not there. But she knew that he was. She knew that he had emerged from a secret place when they first met, and she knew that he would be there now. When she arrived, she began her search.

It was only a few hours from dawn before she found what she was looking for. Had her mind been filled with the greater cultural knowledge concerning hidden passageways, as it would be in later years, she would have found it sooner. She would have immediately identified that what she sought was the candle stick attached to the western wall of the room. It was the only candle stick attached to the wall in the room, and it was clumsily placed in between two large book shelves. No other object in the room appeared to have been placed with such ill purpose. She noticed it only after slumping into the Rabbi's chair out of exhaustion. She had not had any sleep for some time. She propped her feet up on top of the desk, tilted her head back, and exhaled while trying to think of where to look next. It was when she raised her head, after sometime time in thought, that she noticed the strange thing on the wall, poised in between her feet. She got up, advanced to the candle, examined it, and then pulled it downwards. The candle stick, which was attached to a cord, came free of the wall. Startled by this, Tzeitel dropped it. It swung back and hit the wall with a light clank. She quickly knelt down to save the flame on the candle itself, which had tumbled to the floor. After she picked up the candle, its light revealed that a small section of the wooden floor had opened like a hatch, revealing the rickety top rung of a ladder, leading down into darkness. She had to remind herself how urgent her quest was before going down. Taking the candle with her, she carefully descended with a nervous look and a gulp.

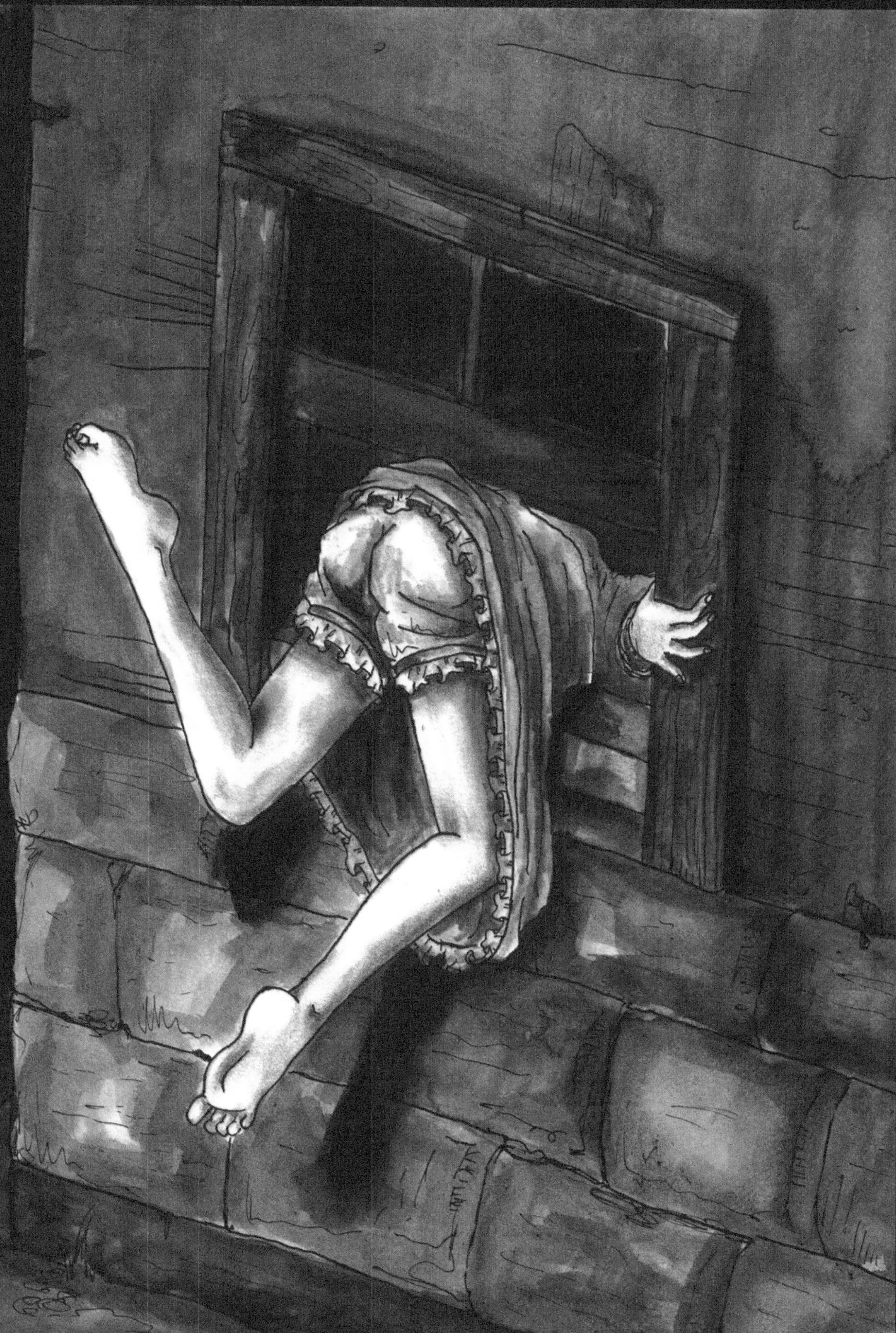

The dim light from her candle illuminated a short cavernous passageway which led to a precarious set of stone stairs. All in all, it reminded her of her first journey through the cave in the forest. This sense of nostalgia was only heightened when she began to hear someone chanting. Just like she had with Avi's voice, she followed this one to an old wooden door. Even though the voice did not match, her heart ached with the hope that she would find her lost companion on the other side.

But Tzeitel was no fool and knew better than to barge through a strange door with strange chanting coming from the other side. This time she could not tell what she would find and, as such, was not afforded the opportunity to mull it over. She crouched down low enough to peer through the keyhole, but it revealed nothing to her. With nothing left to do, she crouched down even further and slowly turned the knob of the door. She was for once in her life grateful for being too poor to own a pair of shoes, as her soft bare feet allowed her to advance into the room in complete silence.

Immediately as she entered, she was faced with a large bookshelf filled with a few old volumes, a skull, and objects that she had never even dreamed of. Her attention then returned to the chanting which had continued after a brief pause. The words sounded like Hebrew, but she could not understand them. As she listened, she began to pick out one word that continually re-peated. Although this word was among the ones that she did not know, her instincts told her that normally, such a word should not be spoken. She rounded the corner of the bookshelf when the chant began to consist of only that word.

Her quiet feet continued to carry her through the most stealthful of approaches until the chanter came into view. It did not surprise her that it was the old Rabbi. What did surprise her was what he was doing and what he was doing it to.

The Rabbi was reading his chant from his old tome that contained the drawings of Avi. While he chanted, standing atop a stool, he used an awl to engrave the word "emet" upon the forehead of a towering, motionless creature standing in the middle of the room. This creature was unmistakably her lost companion, who, as far as she knew, had been left back in the cave. Tzeitel did not have an urge to rush over to the Rabbi and demand to be told what he was doing. The ritual she was witnessing had enthralled her young curiosity, and she waited with an almost unbearable anticipation for what would happen next.

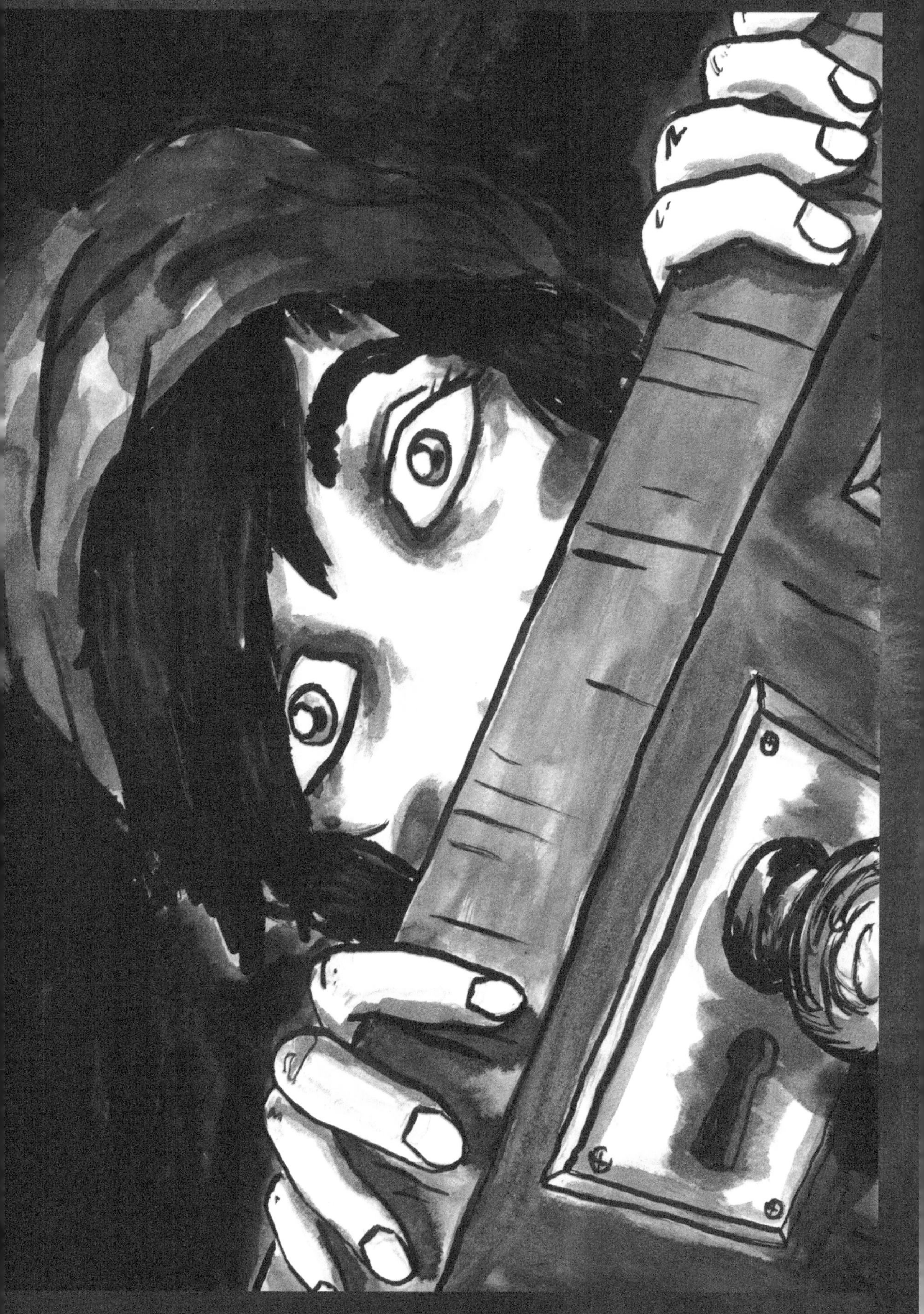

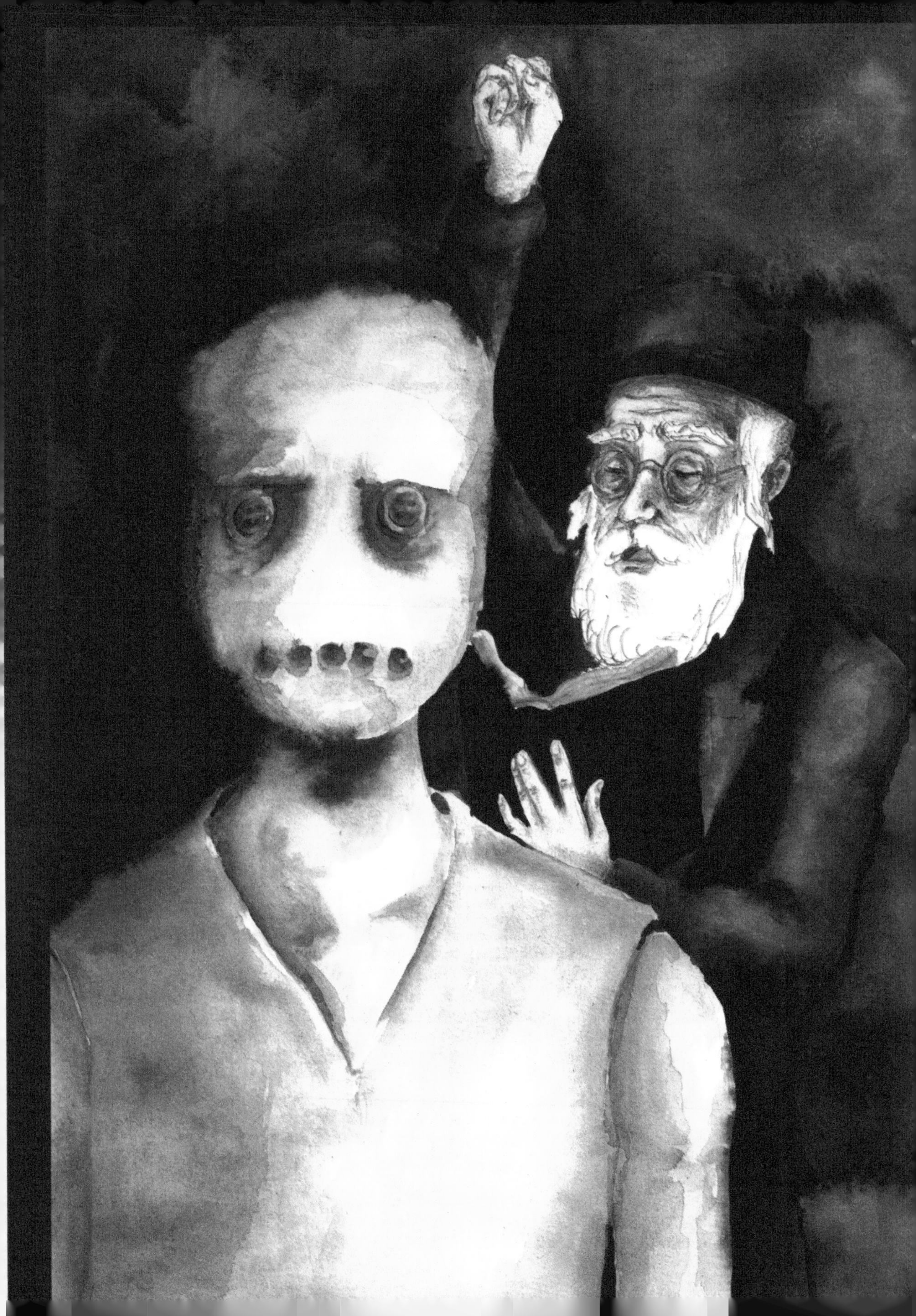

With a few final words of the chant, the Rabbi completed inscribing the Aleph. With that, he dismounted his stool as the creature began to shift in place. The Rabbi took a few steps back and a few to the side so that he was standing (what he considered to be) a safe distance away. He was positioned in front of the creature and asked it, "can you understand me?"

The creature said nothing, so the Rabbi asked again, and still the creature did not speak.

As the Rabbi continuously attempted to address the golem, it, too, continued to sway in place. Its head began to move as it began to look around the room. Tzeitel grew worried as the Rabbi's demands grew in intensity. But his demands sounded more like impassioned requests, and his tone sounded more like that of a desperate man pleading for his life. It seemed as if the Rabbi would break down into tears at any moment. Still the golem would not answer him, and Tzeitel let her guard down which caused her to unintentionally shift in place and knock against another bookshelf. A phial containing an unknown liquid fell and shattered against the stone floor. The liquid sizzled as if it were being poured onto a hot skillet. This caused both the Rabbi and the golem to come to full attention and divert it to the corner which Tzeitel occupied. She was caught. The Rabbi's face grew livid with anger and he began to storm over to her, but was stopped dead in place when the golem spoke.

"Little one," it said looking directly at the frightened Tzeitel, "it is strange that even though I do not know who I am, where I am, or why I am here, you seem entirely familiar to me."

The Rabbi turned around in the purest form of bafflement at the creature's words, and then whipped his head around back to Tzeitel. She was standing timidly, holding her hands in front of her, with her head down and gaze forward.

"Avi?" she asked weakly.

The golem took a step forward. "Is that what I am called?"

"It's what I call you."

"Do others call me something different?"

"Yes, but I do not know what those names are."

"What are you called?"

"Tzeitel."

"It's a lovely name."

The two smiled at one another and said nothing for some time. But within that time, they both slowly moved towards one another. The golem did so out of a longing for companionship and love after being born into the world without so much as a "welcome." Tzeitel moved forward out of a longing for the new friend she made and lost. This Avi, despite the fact that he may have been different, was more familiar to her than anything else she had encountered in that new world. When they finally stood directly in front of one another, the golem knelt down and Tzeitel wrapped as much of her arms around it as she could manage. In turn, it drew its massive hands around her and gently placed them over most of her body.

All the Rabbi could think of doing was sitting down. He found a nearby chair and did just that.

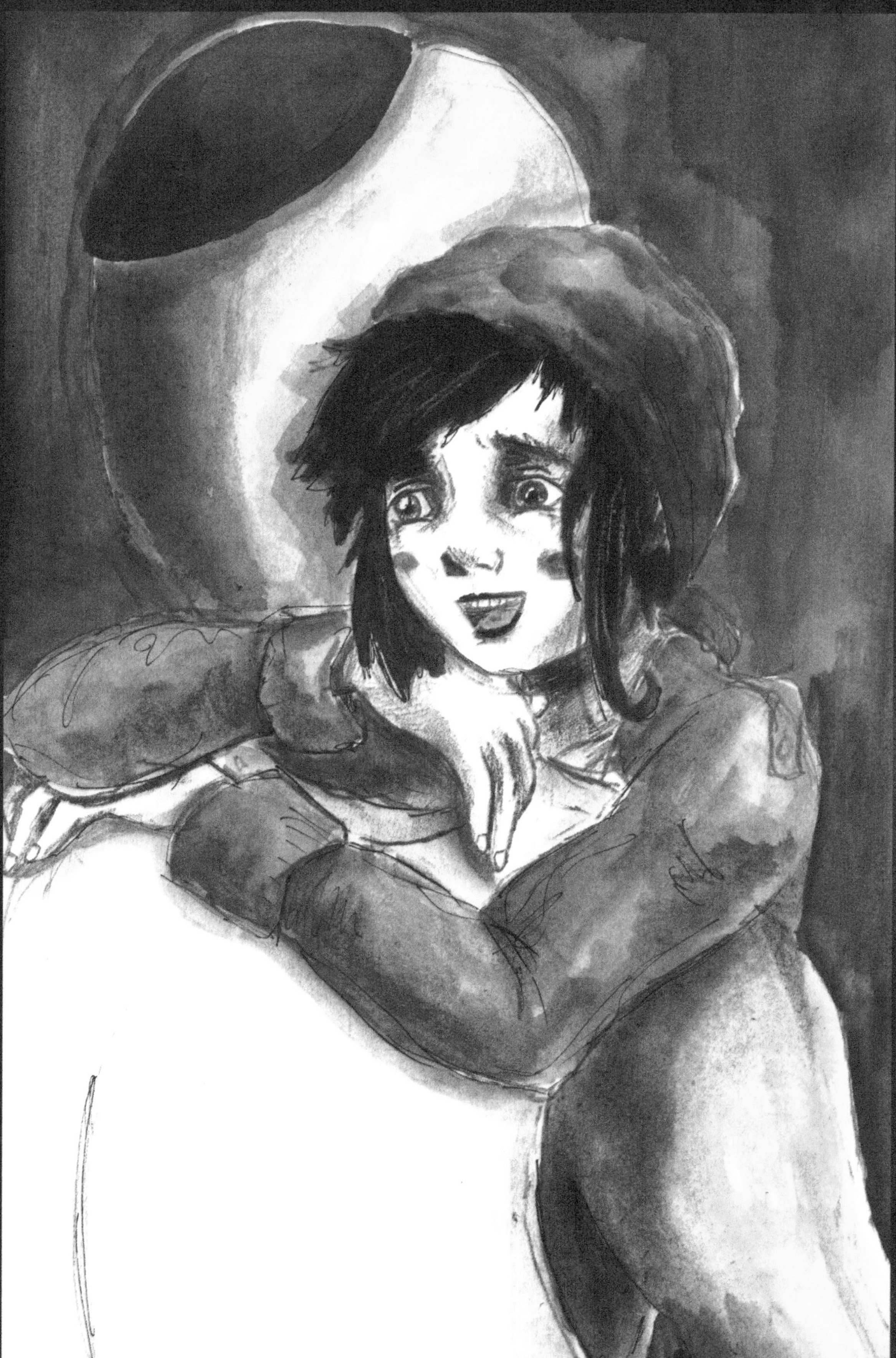

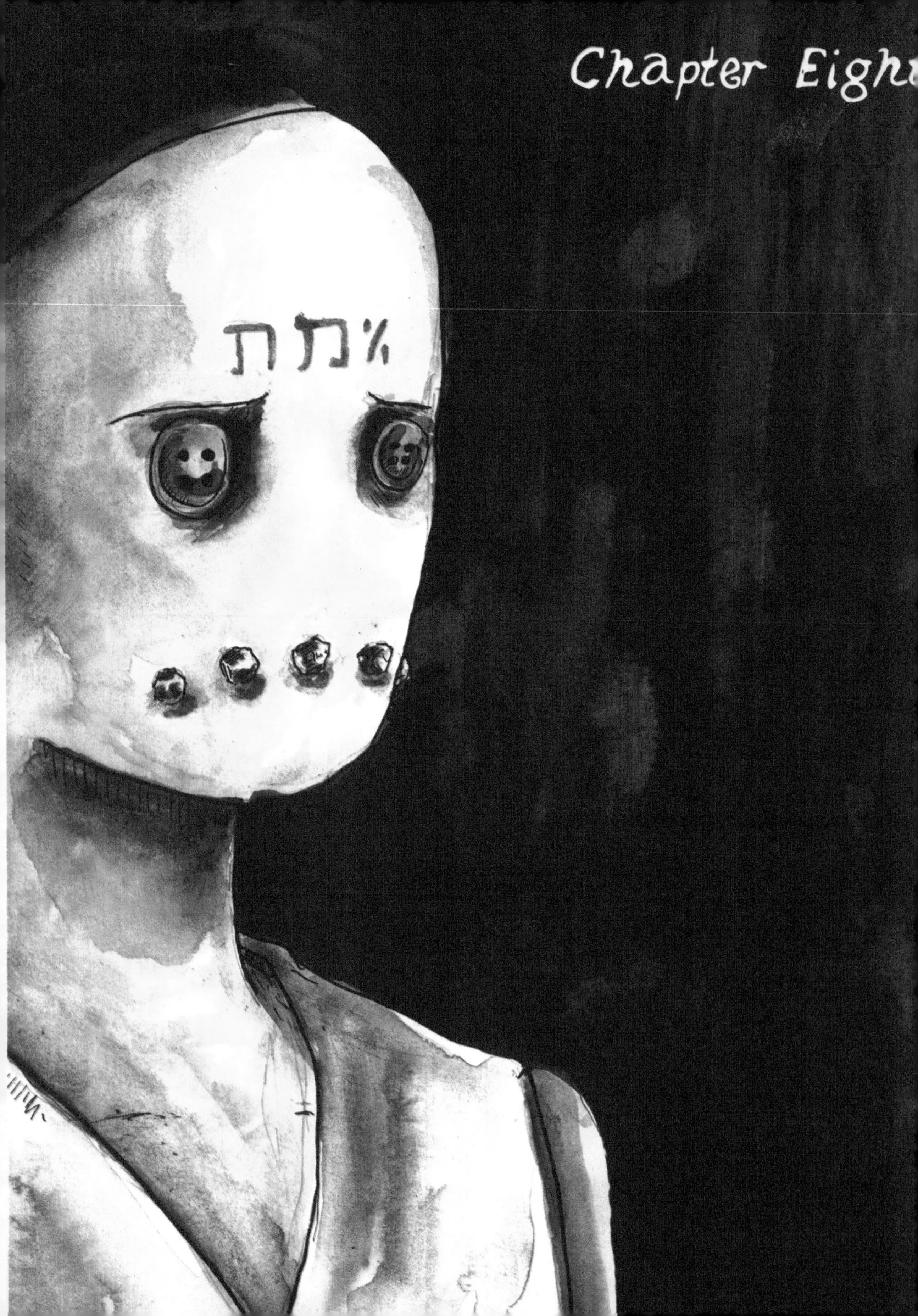
Chapter Eigh
אמת

This event had severely complicated almost every facet of the Rabbi's life. Even though he knew it was a cruel thing to do, he had hoped that Tzeitel, the girl who knew his secrets, would have given up and left. In the back of his mind he of course understood that she would not, but all the same—he hoped.

It was true that even though her story had made little sense, she had been telling the truth. He did not know how, but she knew this creature that he had just given life to. Perhaps she was sent by G-d to help him and his village.

But perhaps not, one must always consider every possibility.

Still not knowing how to proceed, the Rabbi continued to sit in silent contemplation as he watched the scene unfold. The girl and his creature had broken from their embrace and were talking.

"What happened to you, Avi?" Tzeitel asked as she tried to hold his hands.

"I was born—I think."

"But what about the cave, and the pool?" she asked desperately.

"I'm sorry, little one," the golem answered, "I do not know what you mean."

"You don't remember?"

"I don't think I can remember. All my memory consists of are the last few minutes."

"You don't remember rescuing me from freezing to death in the snow? You don't remember first speaking me as you hung my clothes out to dry? You don't remember saving me from the angry spirits? You don't remember my bath in the pool? What about the cave? The village? How you believed that you failed G-d?"

The Rabbi heard her final words, and as she broke down in tears, an intense devastation enveloped his heart. He shot up out of his seat and exclaimed: "failed G-d?"

Tzeitel continued to cry into the golem's arms.

"Child, child," the Rabbi begged, "What did you mean when you said, 'failed G-d'?"

"I don't know," she wept, "He didn't remember."

The Rabbi's heart continued to sink slowly and painfully into his stomach. "Please, child, what do you mean?"

"I don't know what I mean!" Tzeitel screamed in between sobs. "He didn't remember. I think it had something to do with this village."

All at once the Rabbi's research came flooding into his mind. All the accounts and stories of golems turning on their masters and going on a rampage he had read became his only thoughts. He knew the dangers involved, but he knew that he was creating such a thing for good. Would G-d still punish him for meddling in divine affairs? He slowly inched back over to his stool, where his awl sat almost forgotten. As he did, he tried to keep Tzeitel talking. He would not trade one blood bath for another, and knew what had to be done. He knew the girl's words had been truthful before, so what else could it mean?

"Please," he said, "I know this is hard, but you have to tell me all you can."

"The village in the cave," the girl cried, "It had to have been destroyed in a pogrom. It looked just like this one. It was almost as if I traveled into the past when I came here. To-night I came here to tell you about the rest of the village, where the goyim live. It was the same as the one in the cave with the angry spirits."

"What part of the village?" The Rabbi asked.

"The part where—what are you doing?" Tzeitel had removed her face from the golem's chest to catch a breath of air. As she did, she noticed that the Rabbi had taken the awl in his hand. Its point was sharp and shimmered in the candle light.

"What are you doing?" Tzeitel demanded.

"I'm sorry, child," the Rabbi said, "I know your tale to be true, and if I do not do something, this golem could pose a serious risk to my village and my home. I've made a terrible mistake."

"What are you going to do?" Tzeitel bellowed.

"I'm going to deactivate it. I will not trade one pogrom for another!"

With that the Rabbi made a quick advance to the pair, wielding the awl like a dagger. In a fit of rage, Tzeitel cried out and charged the Rabbi.

"No, no, no! I won't let you kill Avi!"

She tackled him, and in the chaos, as they fell to the floor, the Rabbi drove the awl deep into Tzeitel's shoulder. She broke free from him and pressed her hands to the wound and sobbed uncontrollably. The Rabbi fumbled around for his spectacles and gazed in horror at the innocent child, crumbled on the floor in pain. What had he done?

The cries from Tzeitel however, unleashed something within the golem, and in no time at all, the creature had descended upon the venerable Rabbi, lifting him into the air, its hand around the old man's neck. The Rabbi fought for each breath he could get, but before he could beg, Tzeitel already had already thrown herself about the golem's feet.

"Please, Avi, don't," she wept. "It wasn't his fault, please, please."

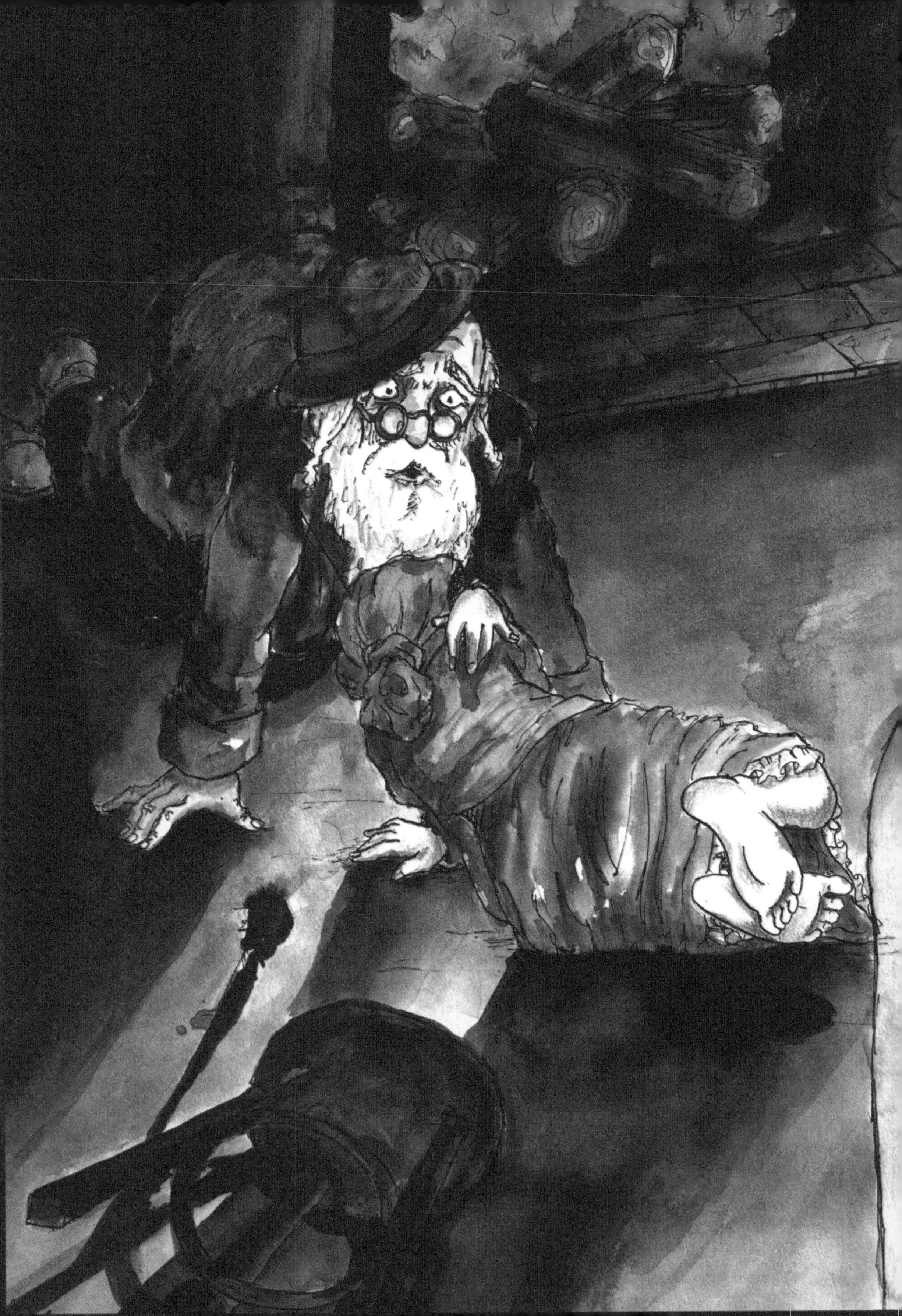

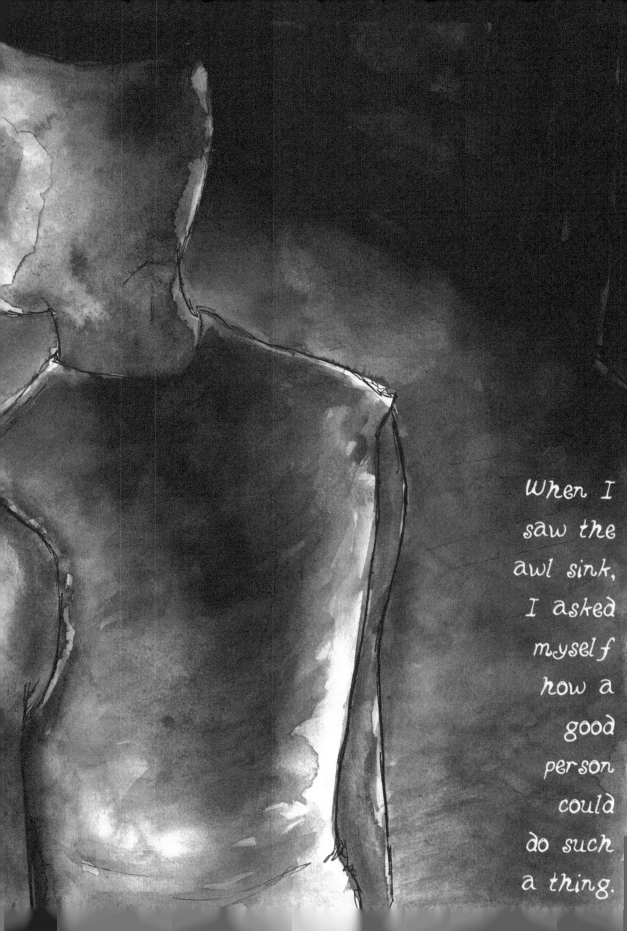

When I saw the awl sink, I asked myself how a good person could do such a thing.

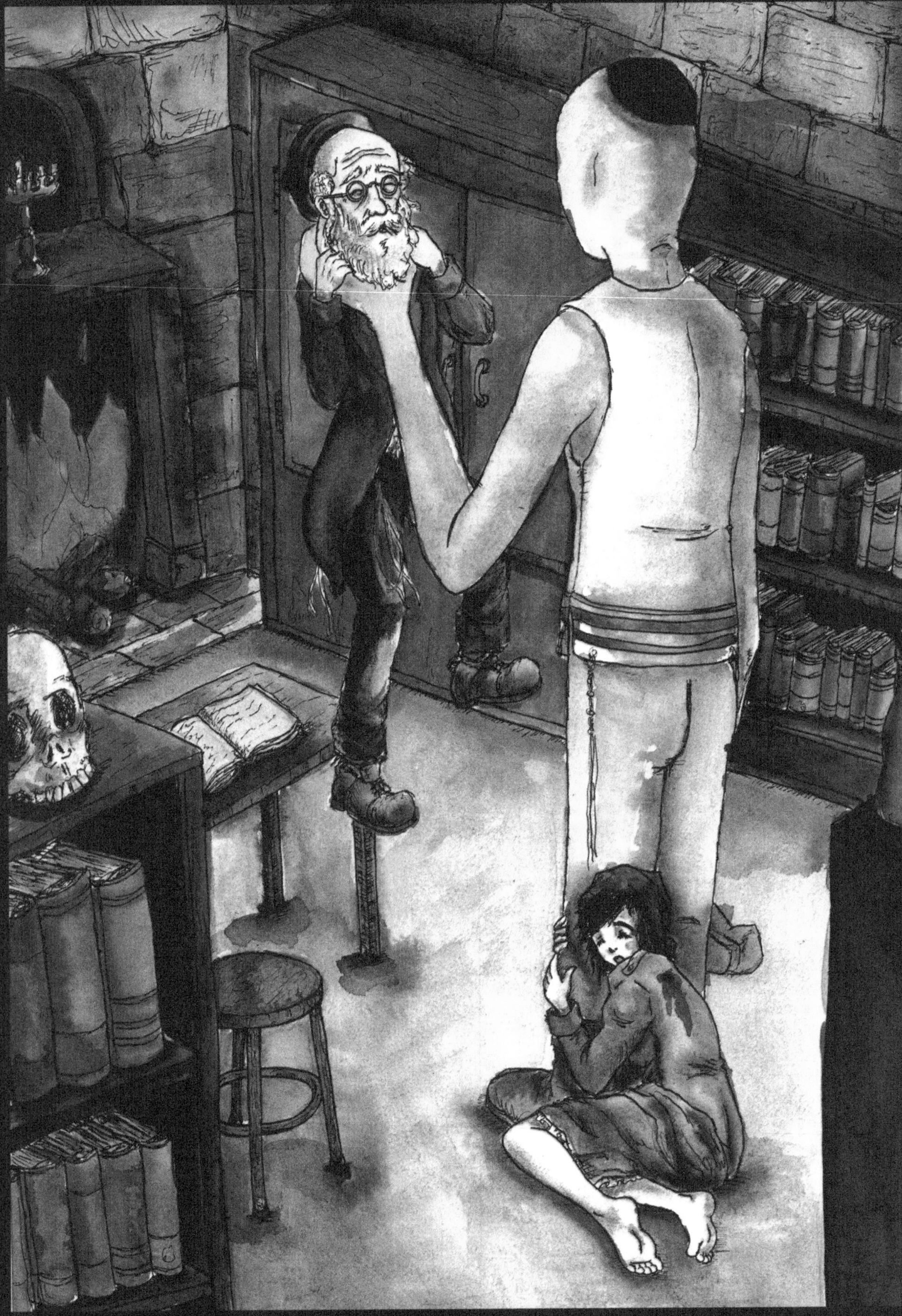

The golem looked down at the fragile child, wounded and crying. He dropped the Rabbi and knelt down to her. Like some other version of himself, he took her up in his arms and cradled her.

"Please, Avi," she went on, her face red and puffy, tears streaming everywhere, "I don't want anyone to die."

Before the golem could answer, the Rabbi had also crawled over. He, too, was weeping.

"I'm so sorry," he sobbed, "I didn't mean to. Please, there's going to be a pogrom here. I don't know when, but I had to do something. I had to do something."

"So you made me?" The golem asked. Both Tzeitel and the Rabbi came to full attention.

"Yes," the Rabbi said quietly as he wiped the tears from his wrinkled face. "You would be able to stop them."

"How do you know that there will be a pogrom?" The creature asked.

"I had heard stories about it happening all over, to many Jewish communities. Rumors spread that it was happening closer. One day I decided to find out if such a thing was being planned for in our village. In my many years of research, I had come across an amulet that granted its wearer invisibility. I took this object and put it on.

After testing it, I made my way among the goyim and entered their police offices. Sure enough, I overheard talk of a pogrom here. They had not decided when, and when it appeared as though they would not have arrived at an agreed upon date anytime soon, I slipped away and began constructing you."

"But what was your intent?" the golem asked, "to have me use my strength to stop them?" The Rabbi bent his head and said nothing.

"Don't you know," the creature continued, "that violence can only create more violence? If I were to stop them, would not they then try to come up with a new way to harm you? Would not there be more?"

"It doesn't even matter anymore," the Rabbi lamented. "This child, who I cannot begin to understand, who knows things that no one possibly could, has said that you will fail G-d." "What does that have to do with anything?" the golem asked. "G-d has no part in the business between you and me."

"But you were created for a purpose," the Rabbi responded. "And apparently, at some point you said that you failed."

"I was created for your purpose." The golem responded harshly. "G-d has no purpose for me. If I have failed at anything its—"

"But you haven't failed at anything," Tzeitel cried. "You saved my life, you became my friend. You're gentle and beautiful; what else matters?"

None of them could say anything. They thought about Tzeitel's words for a long time in silence. And then there was an explosion.

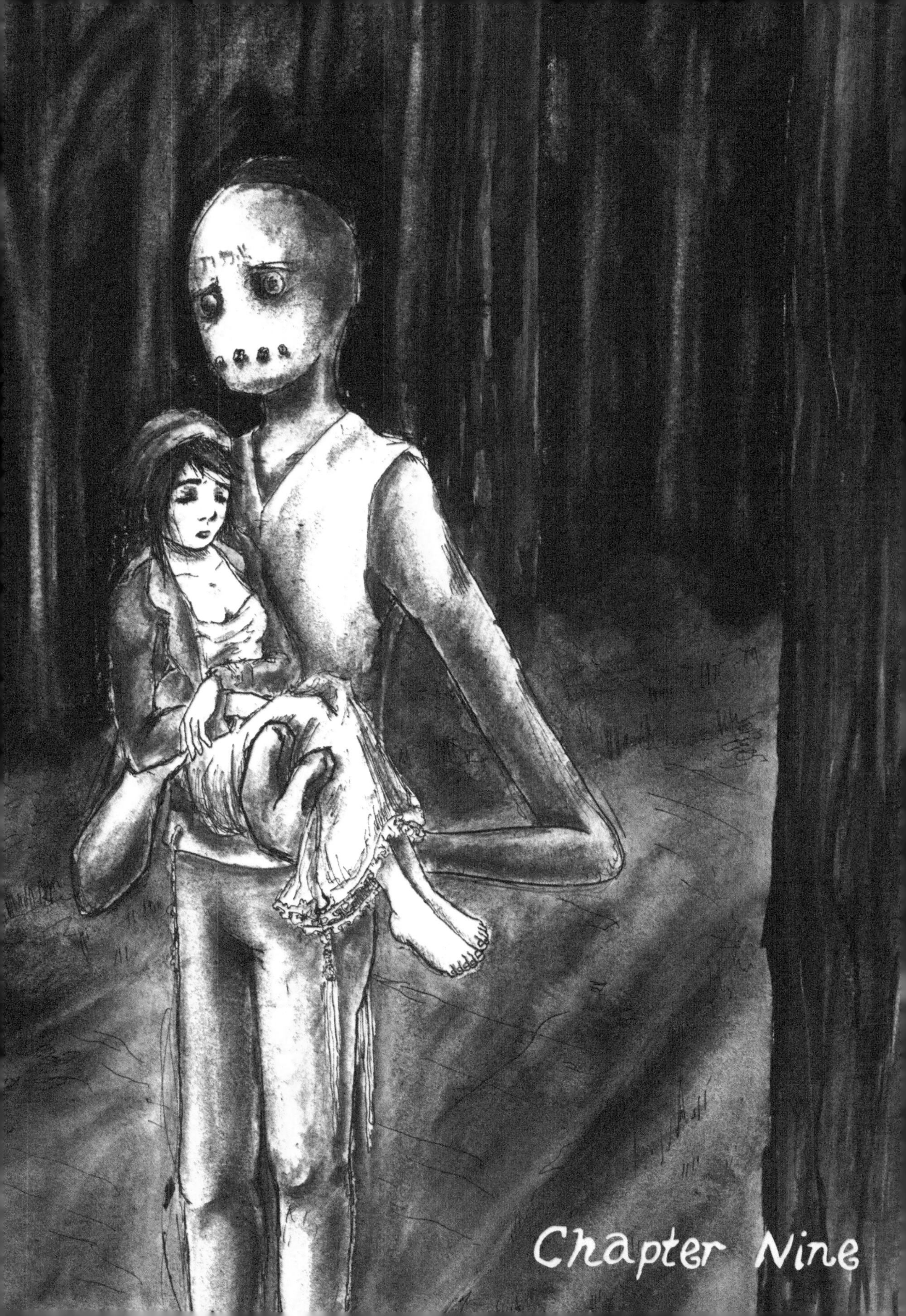
Chapter Nine

Tzeitel did not wake up for a long time, and when she did, she was alone. She slowly opened her eyes and was surprised to find the early night sky staring back at her. She lay in the grass trying to remember how she had gotten there. She remembered Avi and the Rabbi in the secret room. Then she remembered hearing an explosion. Beyond that, like the sky, her memory was clear and empty. She slowly sat up and discovered that she had been lying next to the pond through which she had entered this place. Thoughts of entering it and returning to the cave came into her mind, but she decided against it. Avi had been so different in this world; would he be the same in hers? Would anything be the same for that matter?

Tzeitel made her way up onto her feet and headed off in the direction she thought the village was in. She remembered well, but unfortunately there wasn't much left of the strange little Jewish district when she arrived. It very much resembled what had been in the cave in the forest, only not further worn by time nor buried in the earth. Windows were smashed, doors had been kicked in, and many houses fell in different stages along a scale of partially to completely burnt down. The village really had become a ghost town. Tzeitel discovered no one when she moved among the wreckage much like a ghost herself. She wondered how long she had been asleep, as most of fires had been reduced to embers.

Finally she came to the synagogue and stopped. She stood in front of its charred remains and stared wondering what she would find if she went inside of what was left. She thought back to Avi and the Rabbi and wondered where they were. Tears began to fill her eyes just as someone spoke from behind her.

"I see that it found a safe place for you; I'm glad," the voice said.

"He's not an 'it,'" was Tzeitel's answer to the voice. She knew what it meant. "His name is Avi."

The source of the voice quietly shuffled forward until it stood right next to the girl. It was the Rabbi.

"I'm sorry," the he said. "Sorry for that and many other things."

"You don't have to be sorry," she said reaching an arm around to find that her wound had been cleaned and dressed.

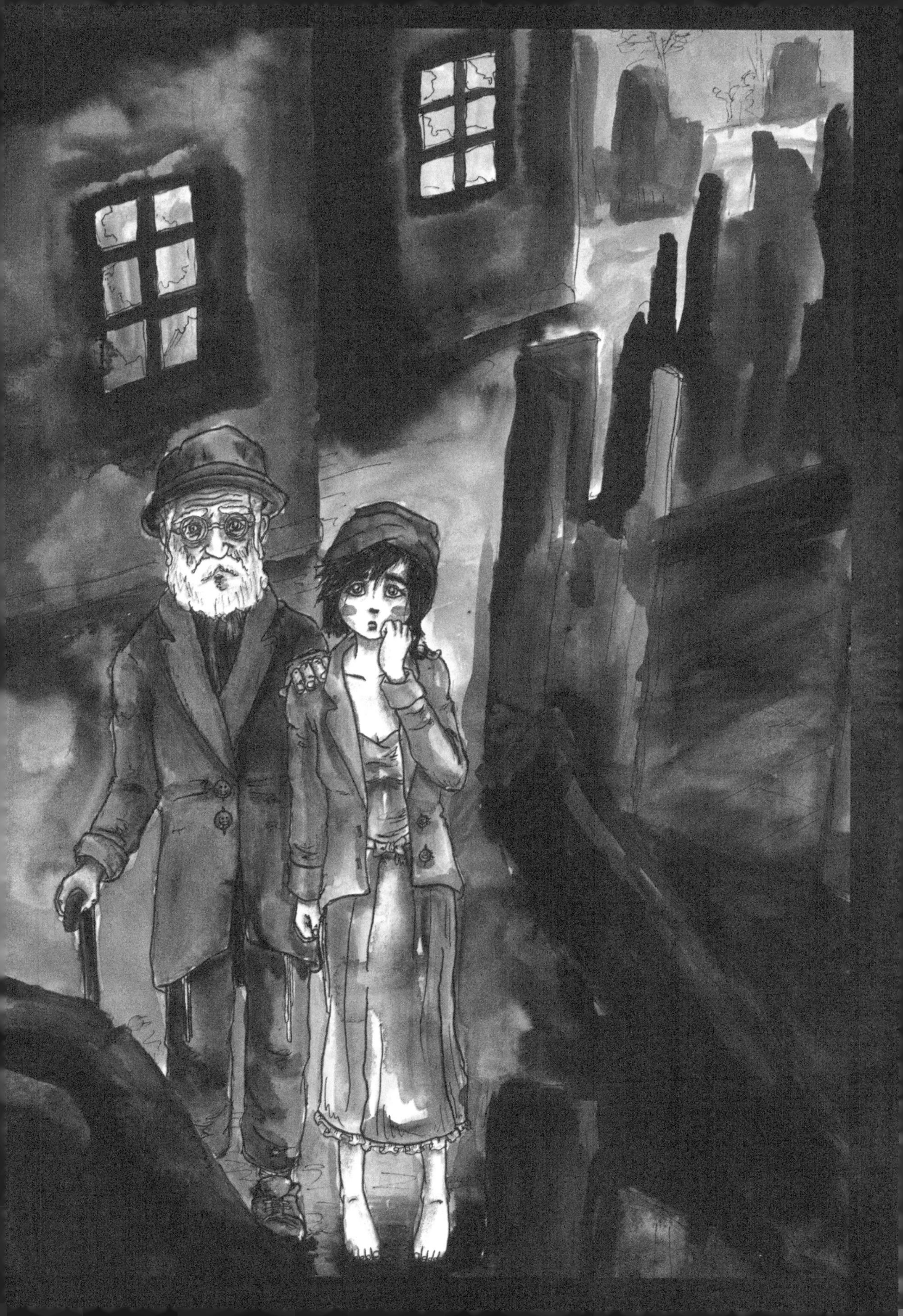

"Well," the Rabbi mused, "I need to take responsibility for my actions. I'm sorry for the way that I've treated you since you arrived. I'm sorry for stabbing you with my awl. If anyone here has failed G-d, it is me."

Neither of the two said anything for a great long time. They only stood and stared at the remains of the village's life.

"Where is everyone?" Tzeitel asked eventually.

"Many have died. I did what I could to tend to the bodies, but I am only one man—and an old one at that. I can only hope that some escaped. Whatever the case may be, we are the last of the Jews in this place."

"Where is Avi?" the girl asked in a sorrowful tone.

"I don't rightly know," said the Rabbi. "I lost consciousness after the third explosion (a bookcase fell on you after the first), and apparently it—um, he—stuffed me in a cupboard that was in my secret room and barricaded me in. I don't know how long I was there—probably a few days. When I did make my way out, he was gone."

"I've lost him again," Tzeitel lamented. She dropped to her knees and clutched her hands together. "Rabbi, why does this happen? What did we ever do wrong?"

"You know," the Rabbi said as he sat down next to the girl, "I've been trying to piece together why he will think that he failed G-d. I mean, that is, if he is the same golem you have met (of which I have no more doubt). Anyway, I've been trying to work it all out, and I think that I've got it. Avi was just born and in the first moments of his life he was exposed to the worst kind of atrocity committable by humanity. Maybe it is just as simple as him not being able to save a whole village. He is a golem after all, it's in his nature to serve and protect his people."

"I guess the world would be a better place if we were all golems then. We'd never want to feel like we failed G-d, so we'd always help everyone," Tzeitel said trying to laugh a little.

"You could say that people are golems. Why do you think that people hate us Jews, or anyone else for that matter? People can be shaped and taught to hate. But the difference between people and golems is that, although you could say that I taught Avi to protect and help, I also taught him violence, even if it was to defend, and he can never unlearn that. G-d gave us free-will and with that, with the ability to stop and think for ourselves, we can unlearn hate."

"But how can people learn to stop hating?" Tzeitel asked.

"Simple," the Rabbi, "the same way anyone is taught anything: by a teacher." With that the old Rabbi stood up and stretched the stiffness out of his joints, "which is just what I am going to do," he said.

"You're going to teach?"

"Yes," said the Rabbi. "I think that I'm going to go out into the world and try and do some good. Maybe I'll find Avi and try to help him; I am responsible anyway."

Tzeitel smiled and stood up next to the Rabbi. She took off her tichel and said, "if you ever see him again, please give him this."

The Rabbi took the cloth and beamed at her. "I will. I take it you're going home then?"

"Yes," she said, "I'm sure that my father and my Avi are very worried about me."

With that Tzeitel and the Rabbi embraced and she gave the old man an affectionate kiss on the cheek.

"Good-bye, Rabbi," Tzeitel said.

"Good-bye, child," he responded. "I'm so sorry for doing you wrong."

Tzeitel turned around and gave the Rabbi a smile. I was one of those smiles that words cannot describe. In it were forgiveness, understanding, and just a hint of a child's cheekiness. I cannot describe it any better than that, but I'm sure that you've gotten the idea.

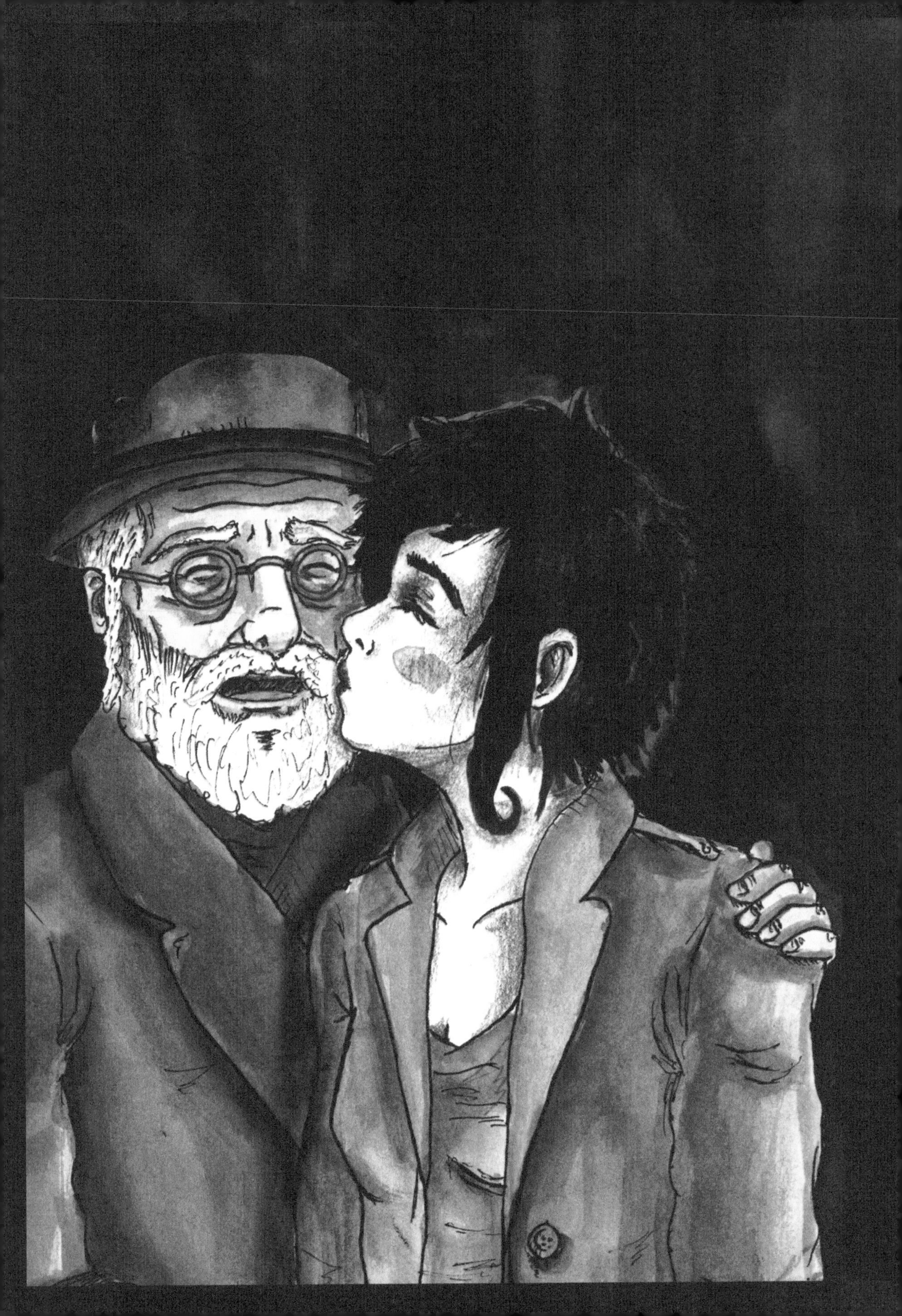

"Oh, Tzeitel," the Rabbi called after some distance had grown between them. Tzeitel turned her head back towards him and stopped.

"I almost forgot," he continued, "I can't for the life of me figure out why or how you came here. Do you have any ideas?"

Tzeitel turned around and, after some thought, shouted back at him, "I don't know how it happened, but I know that it was because I wanted to."

87

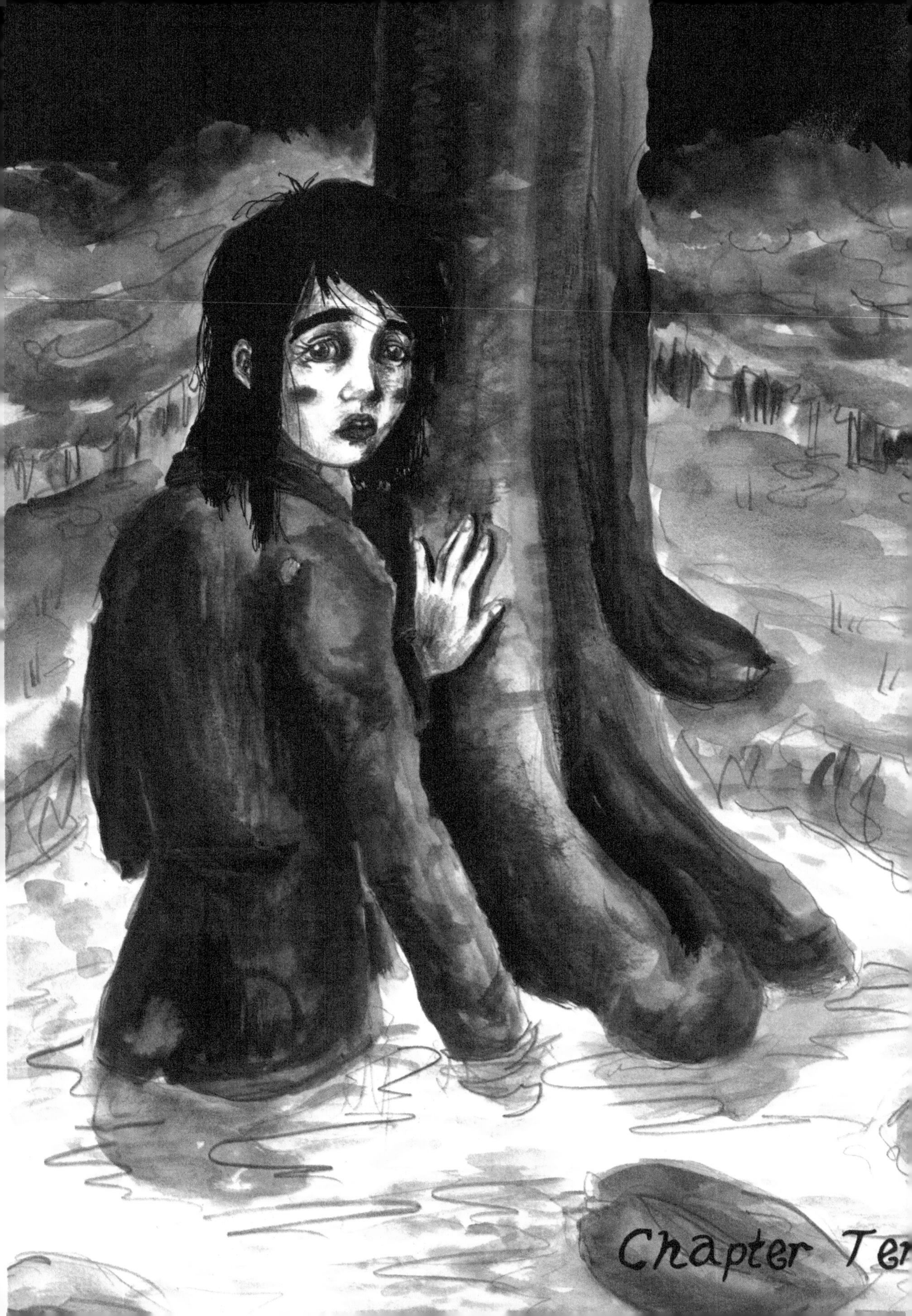
Chapter Ten

After Tzeitel left the Rabbi to his travels, she returned to the pond in which she arrived through and went back in. After a moment, she began to sink and when she did she was not afraid. Like before, for a time she drifted peacefully in the nothingness of the place she was in. She watched the indescribable shapes and masses pass her by, and again, like before, she saw her father. This time she was sitting across from him at their table. They were having their Shabbat dinner on the night that everything began. He complained about how she made the bed sheets dirty from the slush and mud she had tracked in from the night before. He told her that he knew that she was going out into the forest. An argument ensued, and Tzeitel left.

Then everything went black and Tzeitel felt two large coarse and calloused hands covering her eyes. She knew those hands. Then she heard someone say,

"Can I see my surprise now, Papa?"

Had her lips not been moving, Tzeitel would not have known it had been she who spoke. It was not her voice as she knew it then.

"Yes, little Tzeitel, you can see now," came the voice of her father.

Her vision returned, and Tzeitel could see a stuffed bear, made of the finest velvet sitting on the same chair Tzeitel cried in when her mother died. She was six years old; too young to worry about how her father could afford such a gift for her. She turned around and embraced her father.

"Is that really for me, Papa?" she asked.

"Yes, my child, it's really for you."

And just like before, blackness enveloped her and then vanished. Her father's embrace did not end, but as her vision returned, Tzeitel was crying. She was still six years old.

"Why, Papa, why?" she wept, "Why are people so mean?"

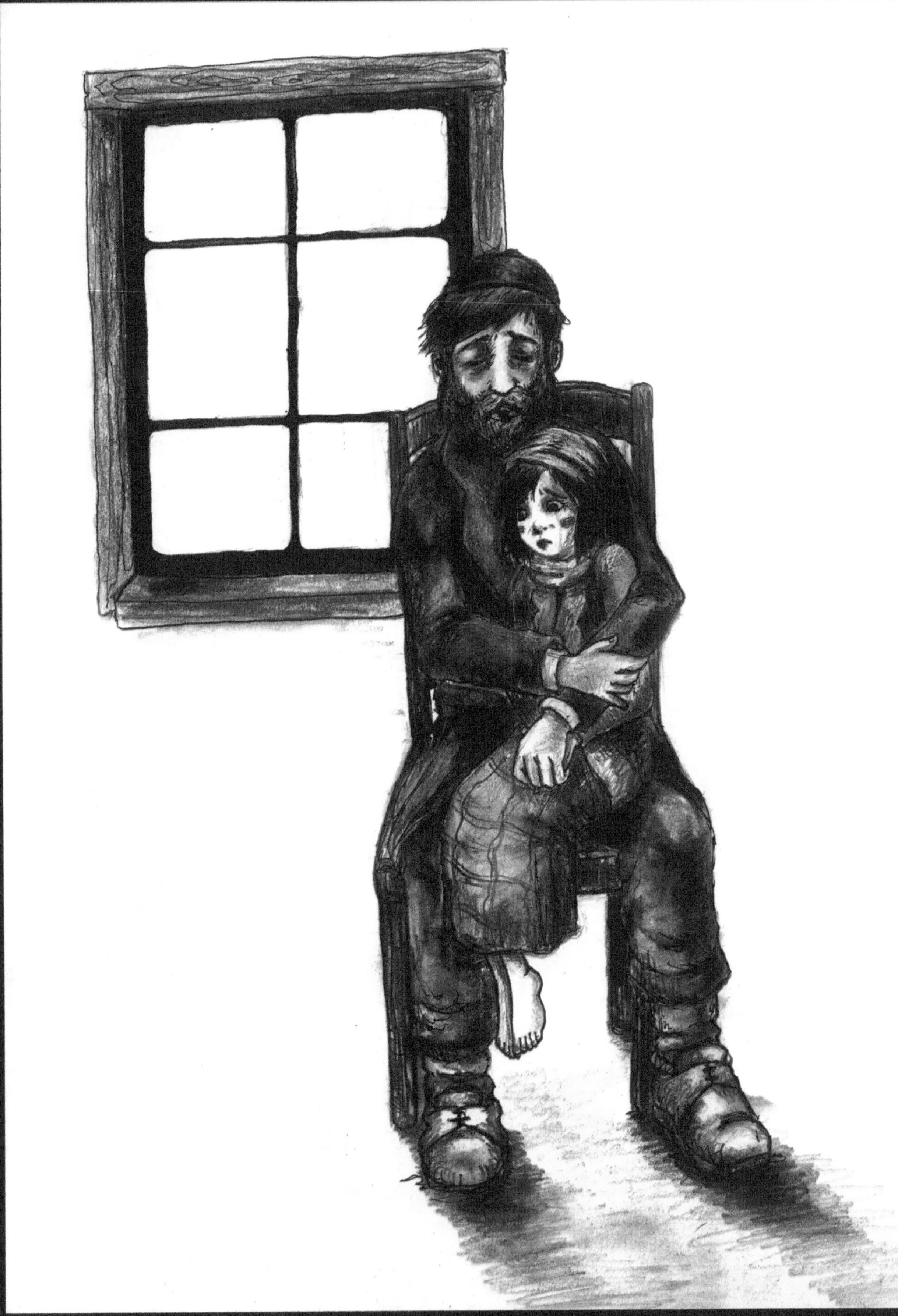

She had just been rescued by her father after wandering alone outside of the Jewish district of their old village. It was there that her velvet bear had been stolen from her and her father had been beaten up for trying to recover it. He held her back and she looked into his patched and bruised face.

"Because," he said, "some people never get taught to be kind to everyone."

"But why?" she demanded through nearly uncontrollable tears. "Don't they have papas to teach them that?"

"I don't know child, I don't know."

Tzeitel felt his embrace again and she closed her eyes causing a fountain of warm tears to gush from them. "Then I wish you could be the whole world's Papa."

When Tzeitel emerged from the pool back in the cave, she wiped the water from her face only to discover that it was still wet from tears. She stood silently in the pool for a very, very long time. Finally, she looked about her and realized that she was back in the cave. She got out of the pool and headed over to the passageway where she had sent Avi so that she could bathe. But when she entered, he was not there.

She wondered if perhaps he had gone about other business because she had been gone so long. After she decided that must be the case, she set out looking for him. She walked the many vaults, chambers, passages, and halls of the cave but still Avi was nowhere to be found. Eventually she decided that she had to check the chambers of the cave that she feared most. She was sure that she had looked everywhere else, and that was the last possible place that he could be. She went there and discovered that no ill will remained stained on there. She walked it freely with no fear, and it was indeed the place where she found the golem, Avi, her friend.

When she found him, she stood in front of him for a moment. Then she turned around and left. She headed back to her father's cottage in the woods—her home, as I know she now calls it. She headed back there and never saw the cave or Avi again, but she still thinks of them often.

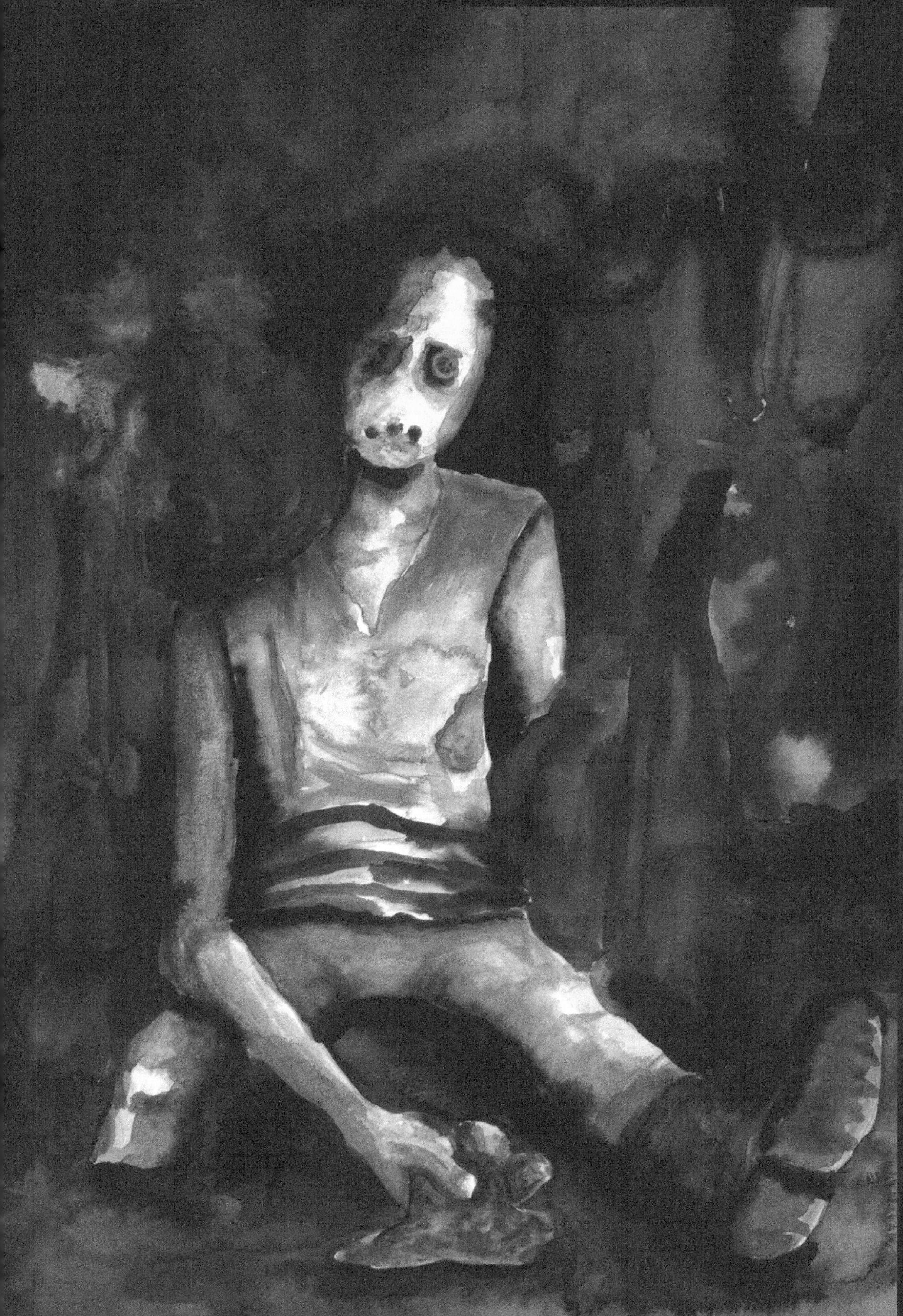

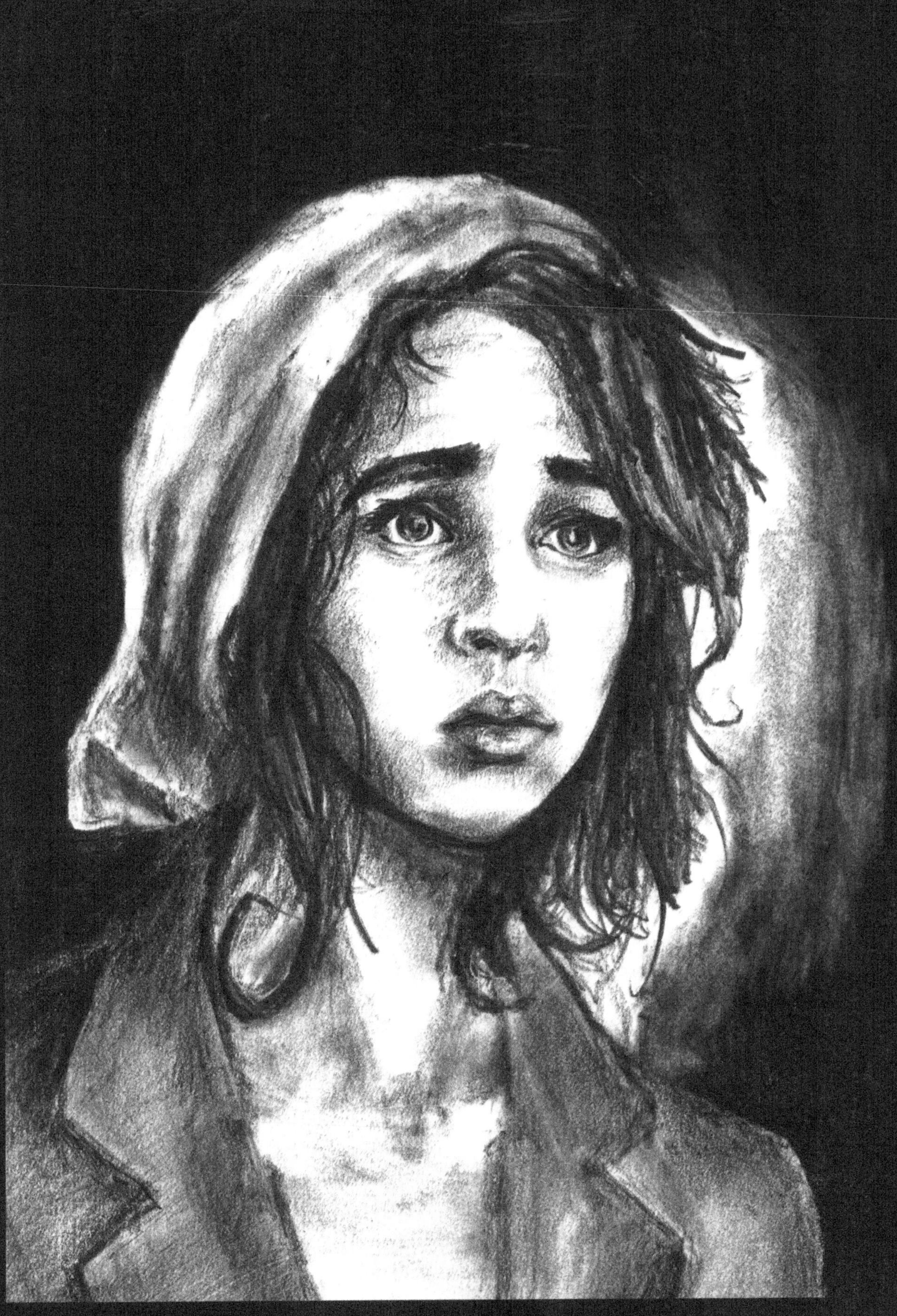

שָׁלוֹם

CPSIA information can be obtained at www.ICGtesting.com
Printed in the USA
BVOW10s2346071114

374070BV00006B/23/P